WELCOME

HOME

WELCOME HOME

MICHAEL O'BRIEN

atmosphere press

Published by Atmosphere Press

Cover design by Kevin Stone
Link to front cover photo credit:
https://commons.wikimedia.org/wiki/File:Plaza_del_Mercado,_Memminge
n,_Alemania,_2019-06-21,_DD_80-86_PAN.jpg

atmospherepress.com

CHAPTER 1

"What was she like, Father?" Peter asked Heinrich as they made their way to the cemetery one Sunday morning.

Peter's father wasn't normally the warm, sentimental type. But something always changed in him when he talked about his first wife.

"I believe your mother was the most beautiful woman in all of Memmingen," Heinrich glowingly told Peter and his two brothers. "She had long, wavy brown hair, big blue eyes, and a warm smile that made you feel as if you were the only person who mattered in the entire world. She made everyone feel that way. And she loved you boys more than anything—you too, Peter. She carried you throughout her pregnancy with great love and anticipation."

Peter beamed with joy upon hearing those words.

Heinrich then paused for a few seconds, surely contemplating the circumstances surrounding the untimely death of his beloved wife, Erna, before adding, "Needless to say, I miss her dearly..." His voice trailed off. He remembered how difficult the first two pregnancies had been for her; as a result, the doctor had strongly recommended that she not have any more children. But they both wanted a large family. Their decision was something Heinrich would have to live with forever.

Peter was born on October 6, 1930, in Memmingen, a small town in Bavaria, Germany, some forty-five miles northeast of the Swiss border. His mother died of complications from his birth the very next day. She had wanted to name their third child Peter, but Heinrich insisted on the name Reinhold instead. Immediately after Erna's death, Heinrich honored her wishes and officially changed the name on the birth certificate to Peter Reinhold Mayer— the lone sibling to have a middle name.

The only real mother Peter ever knew was Hilde, his father's second wife. Heinrich had met Hilde through a cousin of his and married her by the time Peter was two years old. The marriage came somewhat out of necessity because, as a prominent businessman and public figure, Heinrich was hard-pressed to care for a toddler and two older sons under the age of ten.

Heinrich was an astute business owner who worked in the textile industry. A tall, slightly balding man of medium build, he was a well-respected leader in the community. He had his friends and his business, and those two things took up a lot of his time. Everyone knew where they stood with Herr Heinrich Mayer, a strict, no-nonsense gentleman, always well aware of the importance of maintaining a proper image in public. As a matter of fact, he was so particular about his appearance that he would never leave the house wearing anything but a three-piece suit. Except, of course, when he was going fishing. On such occasions, he would remove his jacket and tie and hang them on the nearest tree branch. He would also allow himself to roll up his sleeves, but only in extremely warm weather. As soon as the fish stopped biting and it was time to head home, the sleeves returned to their normal length, and the rest of Heinrich's outfit also fell neatly back into place.

Heinrich remained steadfastly devoted to his first wife, even after he remarried. Every Sunday morning, the family would rise by 7:00 a.m. for breakfast and then attend the weekly church service at Martinskirche (St. Martin Church). Once the service ended, Hilde would return home to begin preparations for the midday meal while Peter and his brothers accompanied their father to the cemetery to visit their mother's grave. This happened every Sunday, without fail. But first, Hilde would dutifully make her way to the backyard garden and pick two bunches of flowers—one bouquet for the gravesite, and the other reserved for a vase in the living room that was placed in front of a prominently displayed photo of Erna. Additionally, all of the household linens featured the monogrammed initials of Erna, and Hilde was expected to use Erna's everyday silver and china, as well. It was quite awkward and humiliating for poor Hilde, but the matter was not open for debate. No doubt, Hilde's was a difficult existence, for even in death, her husband's first wife cast quite a long shadow.

"Do you miss your mother too, Gerhard?" Heinrich asked his eldest son.

Gerhard was eight years old when his mother died, so the memories he had of her were still fresh in his mind. "Mother was wonderful," he said. "I miss everything about her. But most of all, I miss the time we would spend together after school each day. She would make me a snack—a piece of semmel (German roll) with honey and butter. She would sit with me at the kitchen table while I ate the snack, and we would talk about everything that had happened that day. Then I would go to your study to do my homework, and she would start making dinner."

"I remember her tucking me into bed every night," Martin chimed in. "We would sing our bedtime prayer together, and then she would kiss me goodnight."

Soon they arrived at the cemetery and made their way in through a small iron gate. As they walked down the path to Erna's grave, they passed several other family plots, all beautifully landscaped in honor of the deceased. Because land is quite scarce in Germany, bodies, which are not preserved, are buried in simple wooden coffins that break down over time. Thus, burial plots are leased for a minimum of twenty-five years, and then they are reused by other people.

Erna's gravesite was impeccably maintained—a memorial garden of sorts for the matriarch of the family. Peter's father had purchased a fifty-year lease with the option to extend the term so that he and other family members could also be buried there. The plot, which measured approximately one hundred square feet, was outlined in dark stone and covered in finely ground oak mulch. It featured a variety of plant life, including azaleas positioned in a half-circle around the six-foot-tall granite headstone with a rhododendron bush guarding either side; two rows of small, neatly trimmed yews just inside the vertical stone borders; and several clusters of primroses, begonias, and vincas in the middle. Peter's father had designed it himself, and every time he came for a visit, he would ensure that no branch, leaf, or petal was out of place.

Once the inspection of the grounds was complete, the boys would carry out their assignments. Martin would carefully place the freshly cut flowers into the pewter urn, which was positioned to the left of the headstone, and Peter would fill the urn with water from a small pail he had brought from home. Gerhard would take a small box of matches from his pants pocket and light the short, thick, red candle that was displayed inside a pewter box to the right of the headstone. Then, their father would lead them in prayer. "Our Father, who art in heaven, hallowed be thy name..." After a few moments of silent reflection, the four of them would solemnly depart for home.

By the time Peter turned six years old, his father and stepmother had had two of their own children together: a daughter, aptly named Erna, and a son, Reinhold. This made matters rather difficult for Peter. He loved his younger sister and brother, but with two older siblings from his father's first marriage and two younger ones from the second, he found himself both literally and figuratively caught in the middle.

To his stepmother's credit, she raised Peter as if he were her own. After all, she was the only mother he had ever known. But she also tended to favor the two younger children, her own flesh and blood. Sometimes, either fairly or unfairly, they came first. This may not have been all that intentional, but it was quite obvious to everyone watching. So, perhaps out of anger and resentment, Gerhard and Martin grew defiant of Hilde over time, especially in their father's absence, which created quite a bit of tension in the household. This put Peter in a tough spot because, in his heart, Hilde was his mother, his primary caregiver, and his maternal influence. And Gerhard and Martin were his big brothers, his protectors, and his role models.

This issue certainly wore on Peter as he grew older, causing him much stress and anxiety along the way. It also set the stage for what would ultimately become the biggest decision of his life.

CHAPTER 2

Upon returning from the cemetery one day, Peter entered his house to the sound of laughter coming from the drawing room, where his younger siblings, Erna and Reinhold, were playing a game with matchsticks. The object of the game was to successfully remove a matchstick from a jumbled pile without disturbing the others around it. It took both a steady hand and intense concentration, for the players had to ignore their opponents' attempts to distract them while taking their turn. The person with the most pieces at the end of the game was declared the winner.

Peter loved to play matchsticks, and he excelled at it. But, as he watched his brother and sister compete, he knew now was not the time for such fun. Lunch was about to be served. As if on cue, his stepmother stuck her head into the room and put a stop to the game, announcing, "Mittagessen in ten minutes."

With this declaration, there was no more time for frivolity, for the family had a strict schedule to maintain. Lunch, the primary meal of the day, began promptly at noon. This meant that everyone was seated at the table before the clock struck twelve—there were no excuses for being late. Then, a few chores were done, and the family spent some time together. Peter's father came from a close-knit family, with eight siblings in all. Many of them lived within walking distance; thus, they took turns hosting each other on Sunday afternoons for coffee and cake.

Peter quickly helped Erna and Reinhold pick up the game while his older brothers went upstairs to wash for lunch. Then, he followed his nose to the kitchen and checked with his stepmother to see if there was anything he could do to help. As usual, Hilde had everything in hand, but she let him sneak a taste of spätzle while no one else was looking. Hilde made the best spätzle in the world, an egg noodle dish that she served either as a main entrée mixed with butter, melted Swiss cheese, and crispy onions, or as a side dish with goulash or sauerbraten and red cabbage.

Watching his stepmother make spätzle from scratch fascinated Peter. First, she would make sticky dough with just the right combination of flour, eggs, and water. She would always say, "The more eggs, the better. That's what gives it a golden color." Once the dough was kneaded to perfection, she would slap a heaping spoonful of it onto a 6-by-10-inch cutting board specifically designed for making spätzle, and roughly spread it out over its surface. Then, she would hold the board over a pot of boiling water, slice the dough into thin strips, and sweep each strip into the water, all in one motion. True artistry! The noodles would cook for a few minutes and then float to the top once they were done, at which point Hilde would scoop them out of the water and into a bowl to be rinsed. She would routinely throw Peter out of the kitchen at this stage to keep him from eating all that she had made.

If ice cream wasn't available, Hilde would make a special dessert for the family, too. She would send Erna and Reinhold to a neighboring farm for some fresh milk, warning them not to spill any along the way. Of course, with fresh milk, the cream naturally separated and rose to the top of the container. Hilde would use it to make whipped cream, add a bit of sugar and fresh raspberries from the garden, and then spoon the mixture into special trays before placing them in the icebox to chill. A few hours later, the family would enjoy a refreshing, homemade treat.

Hilde was a magnificent cook and a diligent homemaker who took great pride in her work. Short and sturdy, she was also quite reserved, rarely letting herself thoroughly enjoy any moment at hand. There was always something to do, something to clean, or a meal to prepare. It was her duty to maintain the household, and she never disappointed.

Naturally, Hilde's kitchen functioned as her domain, and her coal-burning cast iron stove was the centerpiece of it all. Coal not only powered the cooking operations, but the steam radiators that heated the house also required coal to fuel the boiler. So, the boys would take turns hauling buckets of coal from the cellar up to the kitchen on a daily basis to keep up with the demand. While other families typically had to shop for groceries every day and keep them cool by storing them in the cellar, the Mayers had access to blocks of ice through the family brewery. They were one of the few folks in town to have an icebox in their home.

The kitchen also featured a lovely oak dining set tucked into the back-right corner of the room. Bench seating, fashioned after church pews, adorned two sides along the exterior walls, while four complementary chairs completed the set around the remainder of the table. A beautiful crucifix, hand-carved out of maple, was displayed prominently in the corner, watching over the family meal. Peter so loved the look and feel of this setting that he replicated it in his own home many years later.

As the family gathered around the table for each meal, they held hands and, in unison, prayed in thanksgiving: "Come Lord Jesus, be our guest, and let thy gifts to us be blest. Amen."

Then, they would add a little extra cheer to the moment by swinging their clasped hands back and forth in unison while breaking into a brief song: "Happy is the family meal; I hope you all enjoy the food!"

They would end the chant with one huge clap of their hands.

This ritual, of course, seemed a bit out of character for Heinrich, the stern patriarch of the family. However, it became a pre-meal ritual—a practice started by Peter's birth mother and carried on by the Mayers long after her death.

"Mother, who are we visiting for coffee this afternoon?" Peter asked Hilde one day.

"Onkel Friedrich and Tante Gisela," she replied.

"That's great!" exclaimed Peter, for he always looked forward to visiting Friedrich and Gisela's house. He adored his aunt and uncle, and loved to spend time with their three children: twin brothers Ernst and Josef, and their sister, Gudrun. Peter knew that a fun-filled afternoon was ahead.

Whenever the families came together, the adults held court in the dining room while the older children played cards in the parlor. Sechsundsechzig (Sixty-Six) was their game of choice, and they would play with two, three, or four players. Peter would usually team up with Josef, and Ernst would partner with Gudrun. The object of each hand was to be the first team to collect sixty-six or more card points. The winning team maintained bragging rights until the next visit.

Onkel Friedrich was president of the town's brewery, while Peter's father, uncles, and several cousins served on the company's board of directors. The business started in the late 1800s when Peter's grandfather, Rudolf Mayer, owned a restaurant in Memmingen. Back in the day, each restaurant brewed its own beer. Rudolf's restaurant was known as the Weisser Hengst (White Stallion), and it also supplied beer to a garden-style eatery operated by Peter's grandmother. Eventually, Rudolf's sons ran their own restaurants, as well. Rather than manage all these separate brewing operations, Peter's grandfather decided to consolidate and form a larger and more efficient operation. So, they established the Weisser Hengst Brauerei (Brewery). Over time, Weisser Hengst grew even larger by buying out other restaurants and ultimately became the primary brewery in all of Memmingen, supplying beer to most of the major eating and drinking establishments throughout the region.

Weisser Hengst had become the family's legacy, a point of pride and responsibility that every Mayer took seriously. Peter's father and the other directors would strive to frequent each local establishment regularly for either dinner or a few beers, as a way to thank the owners for serving Weisser Hengst products.

One particular evening, Peter joined his father and uncles at a client's restaurant for dinner. After taking a few bites of his meal, Peter whispered to his cousin Josef, who was sitting next to him, "This tastes awful." Josef nodded and cringed in agreement as Peter made eye contact with his father across the table. His father's cold, icy stare clearly said all that he needed to know: *Quiet! Don't you dare make a scene, and finish every last bite on your plate.*

Peter then noticed that Onkel Friedrich had already finished his meal without issue. *How could he eat such horrible food, and so quickly?* he wondered. *I guess if he can do it, I have no excuse.*

So, Peter dutifully choked down the meal, bite by sour bite, so as not to embarrass his family or, more importantly, the host. But little did he know that, when no one was looking, Onkel Friedrich had wiped his plate clean with his handkerchief and stuffed all that had been on it into the pocket of his suit jacket. This was quite a feat, considering that the meal consisted of small chunks of beef and dark brown gravy. Unfortunately, Tante Gisela didn't find out about what her husband had done until days later when she took the suit to the cleaners. What a dreadful mess!

Another time, Peter accompanied his Onkel Friedrich and cousins Ernst and Josef to a lovely inn and restaurant in the foothills of the Alps. The manager of the restaurant greeted everyone and asked, "Would you like to meet Albert Einstein? He is outside in the biergarten."

Despite his youth, Peter lit up with anticipation. He had heard about the renowned achievements of Dr. Einstein from his father.

Of course, no one wanted to pass up this golden opportunity, for the man was as close to German royalty as one could get. "It would be an honor!" replied Onkel Friedrich, trying to contain his enthusiasm as the boys murmured to each other with delight.

When the Mayers reached the biergarten, they could see Dr. Einstein sitting alone at a table, enjoying a Weissbier, and gazing into the sky, appearing deep in thought. Onkel Friedrich stopped in his tracks, extended his arms to his sides, and motioned for the boys to back up. "I don't think we should bother Herr Doktor today," he whispered to the restaurant manager. "It looks as if he has more important things on his mind. However, I see that he is enjoying a Weisser Hengst beer. Please put his bill on my account."

"Yes sir, Herr Mayer," the manager replied. He then seated the Mayers at a table.

About thirty minutes later, the manager returned and tapped Onkel Friedrich on the shoulder. "Excuse me, Herr Mayer. There is someone here who would like to meet you."

As Friedrich turned to acknowledge the manager, Dr. Einstein stood before him. "I understand that you paid my bill today," he said to Friedrich. "What a pleasant surprise, sir. Thank you for the kind gesture."

Caught off guard, Friedrich sprung to his feet to introduce himself and the boys to Dr. Einstein. "It is my pleasure, Herr Doktor! It is an honor to meet you. Do you have business in our region?"

"I am speaking at a conference in Stuttgart tomorrow, and I wanted to enjoy some quiet time away from the city. This was the perfect setting," Dr. Einstein replied. "Thank you again. I hope all of you have a good day." And off he went.

Friedrich marveled at how cordial the man had been, considering his worldwide fame. "What a gentleman," he said to the boys. "And to think I was worried about approaching him!"

* * *

While visiting his aunt and uncle's house for afternoon coffee one day, Peter noticed that the mood was different than normal. Usually, his father and uncles would carry on a spirited discussion about the state of the brewery or topical issues facing the community. But this time, the conversation seemed more muted and somber.

As they walked home, Peter couldn't help but mention what he had noticed. "Father," he began, "What were you talking about today with Onkel Friedrich and Onkel Klaus? Is something wrong?"

His father stopped and turned to him, his face empathetic. "We were discussing what happened near the marktplatz on Wednesday night. But not to worry, everything is going to be alright."

Of course, he was talking about Kristallnacht (the Night of Broken Glass), the main topic of debate in German restaurants, shops, and workplaces over the past several days. Although he was only eight years old at the time, Peter was keenly aware that something horrible had happened in Memmingen on the night of November 9, 1938. A demonstration near the local synagogue had turned violent. Several Jewish-owned businesses were looted, and others were completely destroyed as part of a wave of mob riots that had broken out countrywide after the shooting death of a German diplomat by a Polish-Jewish student.

At the end of the Mayers' block lived two Jewish families, the Güenzburgers and the Laubheimers. On Kristallnacht, though Peter and his family were not aware of the details at the time, they could hear quite a disturbance taking place down the street. Someone had broken into the Güenzburgers' home and completely ransacked the place. They broke windows, destroyed furniture, flung a large crystal vase at a mirror in the foyer, and smashed dishes, glasses, and anything else of value throughout the house. Fortunately, the family was not home at the time.

Upon hearing the commotion, Peter's Onkel Friedrich raced from his home down the street to confront the ruffians, declaring that the Güenzburgers were outstanding members of the community and that their home should be spared. "The owner of this house, Mr. Güenzburger, is a German war hero and a well-respected business owner," he shouted. "He earned a bronze medal of valor during World War I. Leave this honorable man and his family alone. They have done nothing to deserve this brutality." The mayor of Memmingen soon joined in Friedrich's pleas, and, thankfully, the unruly crowd backed down and eventually began to disperse.

Peter and his family lived only a few blocks away from Memmingen's only synagogue, and his paternal grandparents' home was just two doors away. Needless to say, everyone was quite worried on Kristallnacht. Unfortunately, his grandparents didn't own a telephone at the time, making it impossible to safely contact them during all the chaos.

Suddenly, the Mayers heard a knock at their front

door. Tension filled the air as Peter's father went to answer. It was a neighbor stopping by to check on the family and alert them of what was going on.

"Have you heard the news?" Herr Ziegler asked Peter's father. "There is a major disturbance just south of the marktplatz. It appears someone has attacked the Güenzburger home, too. Quite the commotion! I suggest that everyone stay away from there."

Peter's father knew what he had to do. He ignored the warning, quickly grabbed his hat and coat from the rack on the wall, and flew out the door.

"Are you crazy?" Herr Ziegler shouted after him. "I said it is dangerous out there. Where in the world are you going?"

"To my parents' home. I have to make sure they are safe. Please stay with my family until I return," Heinrich replied over his shoulder as he raced down the sidewalk and through the front gate.

The wait seemed to last forever, but Heinrich returned home safely with Peter's grandmother in tow. His grandfather, as expected, refused to leave the house unattended. They would later find out that no other family members experienced any significant problems during the night's harrowing events. Still, Heinrich's children bombarded their father when he arrived back home with questions about what he had seen out in the street, but he refused to give them details. "Nothing to worry about," he replied. "Get upstairs. It's time for bed."

But young Gerhard's curiosity soon got the best of him. When everyone else in the house was asleep, he and Martin decided to sneak out of the house to see what had happened for themselves. Peter wanted to go, too, but his brothers quickly dismissed him. "You're too young," Martin told him. "Stay here, and whatever you do, don't say anything to Father about this!"

Of course, Peter was much too excited to listen. He desperately wanted to join his older brothers, even if it meant possibly getting into trouble with their father. "Please, Martin!" he pleaded. "Please let me go with you! Gerhard, please! I promise I'll do whatever you say—just let me come along!"

Afraid that Peter's appeals would wake the entire household, Gerhard and Martin eventually relented. And so, the quest began. First, they had to make their way out of the house from the second floor, which was no easy task. Not only did they have to slip past their parents' room unnoticed, but first they had to somehow negotiate the narrow, squeaky staircase along the way.

Gerhard knew exactly what to do, for he had managed to sneak out to meet his friends a few times before. "Don't walk on the middle of the steps; stay to the outside," he instructed his brothers in a stern but hushed tone.

Slowly, the boys crept down the first set of stairs, across the creaky landing, and down the remaining flight—fourteen steps in all. It seemed like an eternity before they made it to the hallway on the main floor, then to the foyer, and out the front door—all the while looking over their shoulders to make sure no one had followed them. Once outside, they breathed a heavy sigh of relief.

They retrieved their bicycles from the small storage shed behind the house and carefully walked them down the long gangway, through the front gate—closing it ever so carefully—and out to the curb. Once there, they hopped onto their bikes and sped down the street toward the marktplatz.

As they approached the street corner, they saw a sea of shattered glass, glistening from the streetlights, scattered across the sidewalk and in the street in front of the Güenzburgers' house. "Careful!" Gerhard warned. "Watch out for the glass. We don't need any flat tires."

Once they had navigated the hazardous terrain and made it to the main thoroughfare, they caught a strong whiff of smoke and realized that the action had occurred much closer to home than they had imagined. They also saw a bright glow just above the tree line to the northeast, which seemed to be coming from the area surrounding Memmingen's only synagogue. Several Jewish-owned shops and businesses were located in that part of town, as well.

"This way!" shouted Gerhard, as he turned the corner and raced up the street. Peter could hardly keep pace with the older boys. The faster they pedaled, the more he fell behind. "Wait for me!" he cried. "I can't catch up! Wait!"

Fortunately, his brothers slowed down long enough for Peter to catch up to them. They then heard a commotion in the distance and soon encountered a young couple who flagged them down and begged them to turn around and go home.

"What are you boys doing out here, and at this hour?" the young man asked. "It's way too dangerous!"

"We live nearby, and that's our grandparents' house," Gerhard explained, pointing across the way. "We're just trying to find out what's happening."

"There's an angry mob intent on burning down the synagogue," the young woman informed them. "Others are breaking into some of the local businesses, stealing whatever they can find, smashing windows, and destroying property. Several people have been injured. Please turn around and go home. It's not safe!"

Just then, a group of five or six young men, armed with metal pipes and clubs, rushed past them toward the crowd gathered just a half-block ahead.

Gerhard looked at his brothers and nodded. Slowly, they all turned their bicycles around and began the short trip back home. As they reached the front of their house, they vowed never to say a word to anyone about their experience.

Later that week, another disturbing incident—this time involving the Laubheimers—shook the residents of Sommerstrasse, the Mayers' street. Mr. Laubheimer was a well-respected physician, and one of the Laubheimer children was a classmate of Martin's. But a couple of days after Kristallnacht, they vanished. A small group of neighbors gathered outside their home in shock, wondering what could possibly have happened to the family. Had they been taken away to a concentration camp? Had they fled out of fear? No one knew for sure, and no one ever saw or heard from them again.

It was clear that trouble had been brewing in the weeks and months prior to Kristallnacht. Although the Jewish families in Memmingen were fairly wealthy, they were often shunned by local merchants and therefore faced difficulties purchasing food and other necessities. So, the Mayer family would load up a small wagon with food and other supplies and go, after dark, to the homes of some of their Jewish neighbors to provide them with whatever they could spare.

Soon, many local Jews, including the Löwensteins—

who lived next door to Peter's maternal grandparents—fled the country out of fear for their safety. Despite the attack on their home and against their neighbors' urging, Mr. Güenzburger and his wife firmly decided to stay put. They did, however, have the foresight to send their two children to safety. Their son, Horst, a friend of Peter's, spent the entire duration of the war in Switzerland and eventually settled in Israel. Edith, their daughter, traveled to Sweden and ultimately ended up in Chicago, where she met Maurice, her future husband. Tragically, their parents were later taken to Auschwitz and did not survive.

The Mayer family had no allegiance to Hitler or the Nazi Party. In fact, Peter's father and uncles refused to fly the Nazi flag until they were ordered to either do so or face the consequences—which most likely meant a trip to Dachau, a concentration camp, perhaps for the entire family.

Peter's Onkel Friedrich knew a man who was sent to Dachau not because he was Jewish, but because he refused to cooperate with or support the Nazi Party. Dachau was located a little over an hour's drive from Memmingen. Fortunately, the man was eventually released without being seriously harmed. Friedrich happened to meet him on the street one day and asked, "What is it like in the camp? We've heard about the inhumane abuse and the extermination of many different kinds of people—Jews, gypsies, and even German citizens! Is it true? Is it as bad as people say?"

In response, the man glanced anxiously to his right and then his left, ultimately refusing to answer the question out of fear that he and his family would be sent back to Dachau—this time, perhaps, for good. "I cannot talk about it—and you shouldn't either if you know what's good for you!" he firmly rebuked Friedrich. Then he dashed down the street and out of sight.

Most Germans, especially those not involved with the Nazi Party, were fairly naive as to the atrocities being committed in the concentration camps. They had heard rumors, of course, but nothing substantial. Openly talking about the camps was considered treasonous and would no doubt bring the wrath of the Schutzstaffel (SS), the inner circle of the Nazi Party, down on the person's entire family.

After the war ended, a list of people from Memmingen scheduled to go to concentration camps was found by local officials, and the Mayer name appeared on that list. While this came as no surprise to the Mayer family, it was still chilling.

These things did not happen in Memmingen prior to Kristallnacht. They represented a radical departure from the normal patterns of daily life, and other questionable signs soon began to surface.

In various youth organizations throughout Germany, including the Boy Scouts and the Evangelical Youth, young men learned the value of hard work and physical fitness, as well as gained a love for the outdoors through camping, hiking, and fishing. Peter and his older brothers had greatly benefited from such experiences.

Now, organizations such as these were being consolidated and taken over by the Nazi Party. Membership became mandatory. With World War II lurking just around the corner, everything was about to change.

CHAPTER 3

Peter awoke to the sharp, clanging sound of his faithful alarm clock. "You have GOT to be kidding," he mumbled to no one in particular. The noise echoed throughout his bedroom, and the more he wished it away, the louder it seemed to get. Finally, he smacked the clock into submission.

It was now four-plus years into World War II, and Peter's life had changed dramatically. His brothers were both serving in the German army, so he now had a lot more responsibility around the house. Every morning, he would wake up extra early, 5:00 a.m. to be exact, in order to have enough time to complete his chores before going to school.

Times were tough due to the devaluation of the Reichsmark, and resources were scarce because the government rationed many necessities, including foodstuffs, clothing, shoes, leather, and soap. Although some items, such as coffee, were not being rationed, they were difficult to come by because they were normally imported from overseas. Luxury items, such as chocolate and whipped cream, had become extinct.

Each household in Memmingen received a monthly allotment of color-coded ration stamps from City Hall based on the number of people in the family. These stamps were used to purchase certain amounts of, for instance, butter, sugar, fruit, grains, and meat. So, if one went to the store and used up all their stamps in a single shopping trip, then they might have nothing left toward the end of the month. The citizens had to be very careful that they divided up their stamps in a shrewd way.

Ration stamps could also be used to dine in restaurants; however, they did not entitle people to handouts of any kind. Everything still had to be paid for. Naturally, the stealing or counterfeiting of stamps was against the law and resulted in detention at forced labor camps.

Everything German citizens did and everything they worked for during the war was about survival. If one raised chickens, for instance, the government allowed them to have only a certain number of chickens based on the number of people living in their household. Additionally, they were required to give a certain number of eggs per chicken to the government. Unfortunately, as the Mayers knew all too well, not every chicken lays eggs on a regular basis. So, they had to manage their supply very carefully, which meant that the government often got eggs before they did. The Mayers had a fairly large family, and it took a lot of eggs to feed everyone. If they didn't have enough, they would sometimes barter with their neighbors and friends.

On a Saturday morning, Peter might ride his bicycle a couple of miles away to visit some family friends who owned a farm. There, he would trade for some milk or a few eggs. He would trade anything his family had, depending on what the farmers needed. The items that the Mayers grew or raised in their garden were just for family; there weren't enough to trade. And the Mayers couldn't risk getting caught by the government buying items directly from their neighbors. But Peter's father was a business owner who sold textiles and other goods, such as china, silverware, and glassware. Sometimes, when absolutely necessary, that's what they would use in their trading.

And they didn't waste anything. Heart. Lung. Brain. It all somehow made its way into a soup or a meal, and the family ate it whether they liked it or not. During wartime, people also got extremely creative in making what became known as "imitation foods" for flour, spinach, salad spreads, and even meat and fish. Imitation coffee became the norm, fashioned from a recipe of roasted barley, oats, chicory, and acorns. Peter fondly referred to it as "kids' coffee."

As the war dragged on, it began to take a major toll on the German people and demanded that a more severe rationing system be implemented by the government. This program made allowances for the working class within the heavy industry sector at the expense of Jews and Poles living in areas occupied by Germany. Eventually, bread, meat, and fat rations were drastically reduced due to a lack of manpower for farming and the increased need to feed the troops and the forced laborers and refugees from neighboring countries.

The Mayer family maintained a garden about a block away from their house. It was a fairly large parcel of land, measuring about 6,500 square feet in size. Many of the more affluent families in town also owned a separate piece of property not far from their house where they could produce food, especially during the war.

Everything Peter needed for his daily chores had to be transported from his house. The family kept a small garden hose with a faucet on their land, but they shut off the water during wintertime. So, first, Peter would use the spigot in his backyard to pump some water by hand into two large containers. Then, he would lift each filled container onto a homemade cart that he had built himself (he was both creative and good with his hands). He would then use a piece of rope to attach the cart to the back of his bicycle before hauling the heavy load down the street and around the corner.

Depending on the season, Peter would water the various fruit and vegetable plants, which included strawberries; raspberries; white, red, and black currants; beans; and tomatoes. The family also had eight large apple trees and a couple of pear trees, as well. Hilde, with young Erna's help, would can the fruits and use them for meals throughout the year.

Finally, Peter would tend to the animals—the Mayer family raised chickens, rabbits, and goats. He absolutely loved animals and struggled to keep from growing too attached to them since, eventually, they would find their way onto the dinner table.

Peter's cousin Josef and his family kept rabbits, ducks, and chickens right in their backyard. A large Brahma rooster, standing nearly three feet tall, watched over all the hens and ducks like a drill sergeant. He interrupted their sleep each morning, herded them out of the hen house, made sure they pecked for worms, and then escorted them back into the hen house at night—including the poor ducks. One time, when one or two ducks refused to get out of their pond at the end of the day, the rooster ventured into the water and bullied them until they reluctantly returned to the hen house. They dared not defy the commander.

Then there was the time when the Mayers were eating their midday meal. The big rooster marched into the dining room and right up to the table. He peered over the edge of the table to see if there was anything for him and his flock to eat and was promptly escorted back outside. He was quite a character, and the family was very fond of him. When Josef and Ernst returned from the war, however, the rooster was nowhere to be found. Food had been scarce. Had he eventually paid a visit to the kitchen table, not as an unwelcome guest, but as the main course? They didn't dare ask what happened to him because they really didn't want to know the answer.

Peter had to carry out many responsibilities on his own. In addition to feeding all the animals, he had to milk the goats, collect eggs from the chickens, and clean out the stable and coop. He also tried to raise bees on his own for a while, but he didn't get much honey from them—only stings, and lots of them. Once he was finished with his morning chores, he'd race back home, get cleaned up, and head to school. In the evenings after dinner, he would do it all over again.

On his way back home from tending to the animals, he would occasionally stop by Herr Ziegler's house and barter some of the eggs and goat milk for butter and freshly baked semmeln. By doing so, the two families were able to help each other out and make what they did have go a little further.

"Guten morgen, Peter!" said Herr Ziegler during one

of Peter's visits. "How are you today?"

"Doing well, thank you!" Peter replied. "The chickens weren't very cooperative this morning, so I don't have any eggs for you."

"That's quite alright, son. And how are your brothers? Have you heard from them lately?"

"We received a letter from Gerhard the other day, but Martin hasn't been in contact with us for many weeks. Father is really starting to worry."

Peter's brother Gerhard had been working as an apprentice at the local Raiffeisen Bank when he was drafted into the army in 1940 at the age of eighteen. He had suffered a severe leg injury when he was about ten years old, which was why he hadn't been drafted right away. He was accidentally kicked by a classmate on the school playground, and the bone marrow in that leg became infected. With no medicine strong enough to clear up the infection, a surgeon had to remove a few inches of bone from his femur. As a result, his injured leg became a bit shorter than the other one. The skin never returned to normal either, remaining bluish in color for the rest of his life.

After his surgery, Gerhard went through extensive rehab at home. The nurse would lay him on his bed and stretch out his leg using a pulley-like contraption. The device consisted of a rope that fed through a wheel attached to the top of a pole. One end of the rope was tied around Gerhard's foot, and the other end was secured to a heavy weight used to pull on the leg. The nurse helped Gerhard perform this exercise for an hour or so every day in the hope that the length of his bad leg would eventually match the good one again. However, it worked all too well;

the bad leg actually became a little longer than the good one.

Martin was serving as an apprentice at the Bavarian Bank when he was drafted at age seventeen and sent to Russia as an Arbeits Dienst (Labor Force) member. There, he supported the war effort through physical labor—mostly digging ditches. Because of their age, he and the other young men in the organization did not participate in active combat. However, they did go through official training exercises, such as marching in parade formation—only instead of rifles, they carried spades.

As soon as Martin turned eighteen, he was transferred to the infantry while in Crimea. He endured an intense three-week training session before joining the 6th Division of the German army in Stalingrad. Unfortunately, he arrived on the same day that the Russians attacked the city. Members of the Italian Division abandoned their post, allowing the Russian troops to encircle and trap the 6th army. Most of the men were either killed or taken prisoner, but about fifteen of them, including Martin, escaped. Martin eventually met up with the remainder of his company, made his way back through Kharkov and Kiev, and wound up fighting in Romania. There, during a fierce battle, he was captured by the Russians and taken to a prison camp back in Crimea.

According to the letters Martin wrote to his family, his Russian captors treated him fairly well. However, everyone in the family, especially his father, was extremely anxious and concerned about his future. This fear only escalated a few months later when all communication with Martin abruptly ended.

Peter looked up to both of his older brothers, but he

especially idolized Martin. Martin was a handsome young man, tall in stature with an athletic build, and he sported dark, wavy hair. He always looked out for his little brother. Even though there were more than six years between them, Martin gladly made time for Peter and developed a special bond with him.

One day, when Peter was just six years old, he and his brothers were playing "Cowboys and Indians" on the front porch of their house. Martin was using Gerhard's air rifle because, even when unloaded, the rifle would make a loud, popping sound when fired, so it was the perfect prop for their game. In full character, Peter was playfully teasing his brother, so Martin responded by shooting at him—not knowing that the rifle was loaded with an actual bullet. The small lead bullet was hollow with a point at one end but, thankfully, had no gunpowder in it. One could crank the rifle and pull the trigger, producing enough force to discharge the bullet. Martin, who was quite a good shot, hit Peter in the nose. Peter started bleeding and soon realized that the bullet had lodged itself inside his left nostril. No one else was home at the time, so Peter never told his parents what had really happened. When pressed for details, he simply claimed to have tripped and hit his nose on a doorknob.

Peter kept the story a secret because he didn't want to get Martin in trouble—or himself, for that matter, since he wasn't supposed to even touch the rifle. But he, in fact, was actually the one responsible for the accident. Gerhard would keep the rifle in a storage closet in Peter's bedroom, unloaded, of course. But Peter was a kid who liked to shoot things, and the temptation was far too great to ignore. So, he would sneakily take the rifle out of the closet whenever he could. From his bedroom window, he would fire shot after shot at the cupula adorning the roof of the next-door neighbor's house. One day, shortly before the incident with Martin, Peter was playing with the rifle when he heard someone coming up the stairs toward his room. Panicked, he quickly stuffed the rifle back in the closet and forgot to remove the bullet. So, ironically, he was the one who had loaded the rifle in the first place.

That night, Martin paid a visit to Peter just after bedtime. "How are you doing, little brother?" he asked.

"My nose is really sore, but I think it'll be okay," replied Peter.

Lowering his voice, Martin then said, "Thanks for not telling Father. That would not have been good. I owe you a big favor. Now try to get some sleep, and I'll see you in the morning." He tousled Peter's hair and headed for the door.

"Martin? Wait. Please don't go yet," Peter quietly pleaded.

Martin could sense that his little brother needed some reassurance that everything truly would be alright. So, he climbed into bed, cuddled up next to Peter, and softly began to sing the prayer he and his mother, Erna, shared every night at bedtime:

It's time for quiet, time for rest.
The day has ended, and I've done my best.
It's time to close my eyes and lay down my head.
O God, please be sure to watch over my bed.

If there was wrong done on this day,
Please, dear Lord, look the other way.

For your Grace and your sacred blood
Make all the wrong become good.

All mankind, large and small,
We are a family, one and all.
Father, keep us safely in your hands,
And help us listen to your commands. Amen.

A sense of peace and comfort came over Peter, and he soon fell asleep.

Even after the bullet wound healed, Peter knew something wasn't quite right. He could feel the slug in his nose and could move it back and forth. But again, he didn't want to say anything about it. Every time he accidentally bumped it or got into a scuffle with another boy in the schoolyard, his nose would bleed. It wasn't until several years later, when Peter was having minor surgery for something unrelated, that he mentioned it to the doctor.

"While I'm knocked out, can you also take the bullet out of my nose?" he asked as he began to drift off to sleep. His doctor, thinking he was joking, simply chuckled and dismissed his request.

When Peter woke up from the surgery, the first thing he did was wrinkle his nose to determine whether or not the bullet was still there. Of course, he was extremely disappointed when he realized the doctor had not removed it.

"The surgery went well, Peter. How do you feel?" asked the doctor.

"My nose!" Peter exclaimed. "I thought you were going to fix my nose, too."

"You were serious about the nose? There really is a bullet in there?"

Peter nodded.

"I can't operate on two different parts of the body at the same time," the doctor explained. "It's just not safe. We will have to take care of it another time." So, Peter had to confess to his parents what really happened to his nose. He returned to the hospital a few weeks later to finally have the bullet removed once and for all.

Ironically, the shooting incident had strengthened the bond between Peter and Martin. So, needless to say, it weighed heavily on young Peter knowing that his brother was facing far more serious trouble now, during the war. *Why haven't we heard from him?* Peter wondered to himself. *It's been such a long time. That can't be good, can it? He's got to be okay. Martin is smart—and he's tough. Maybe he escaped and is hiding out until it's safe. I sure hope so. I just want him to get home as soon as possible. But what if it's not so good? What if...?* Peter wouldn't allow himself to go there in his mind.

"Well, we will keep him—both of your brothers—in our prayers," Herr Ziegler assured him. "Have a good day, Peter!"

When Peter returned to his house, he noticed his father digging a hole in the backyard. "Father, why are you planting bushes so early in the morning?" Peter asked him.

Startled, Peter's father mildly scolded him. "Don't sneak up on me like that," he said. "I am not planting bushes. I just want it to appear that way. It's only a matter of time before the Americans reach Memmingen. When they do, they'll be searching for valuables. So I'm burying ours in the ground. Just a few things, such as your mother's jewelry and some gold and silver coins."

With that, Heinrich lowered a small metal box into the

ground and promptly began to fill the hole with dirt. "The berry bush won't make it so obvious that something is buried here," he informed Peter. "Plus, it will be a lot easier to find again after the war."

Peter admired his father's ingenuity. But the fact that he would take such great measures to protect some of the family's assets deeply concerned him. Would Memmingen be attacked? And, if so, just how safe were they? Over the past few nights, Peter had heard the air raid sirens, so he knew an invasion was possible. He knew that the American forces were nearby. But his father speaking about it so openly and honestly made him realize that the possibility was all too real—and it frightened him like never before.

The days and nights wore on over the next week, and Peter could not get his father's words out of his mind. Each night, before bed, he would hope and pray that his hometown would not come under attack. And each morning, he would awaken to the ringing of his alarm clock. Only now, the sound wasn't nearly as irritating because he knew that it meant they had made it safely through another night.

* * *

A piercing sound interrupted Peter's sleep in the early morning hours of July 18, 1944. This time, however, it wasn't his clock; the alarm was coming from outside the house. "Air raid sirens," he surmised. He knew the drill. But since this was the third night in a row for this disturbance, he felt like rolling over and going back to sleep. "Probably another false alarm," he muttered to himself.

At that moment, he heard his father knock loudly on

his bedroom door. "Let's go—everyone downstairs!" he shouted.

Peter jumped to his feet, grabbed his slippers and robe, and headed out the door, all the while wondering, *Could it be the real thing this time?*

He dashed down the stairs to the main hallway, where he met the rest of his family and a few neighbors who needed a safe place to stay. From there, they hurried to the cellar. Peter's father had converted the space into a bomb shelter. He had reinforced the perimeter with brick and stone and fitted heavy, concrete lean-tos against the windows on the inside for protection from shrapnel. There were also a few mattresses on the floor, a dining set, and several days' worth of food and water to consume if necessary.

"How long will we have to wait down here?" asked Reinhold, Peter's younger brother.

"Until we hear the 'all clear' signal," his mother replied.

Suddenly, they heard a massive boom, and the concrete floor shook beneath them. This time, it was real. Memmingen was under attack, and a feeling of fear and helplessness overcame them all. Peter huddled with Erna at the end of one of the beds. His stepmother held Reinhold in her arms on another bed, while his father and a neighbor moved frantically from window to window to ensure that the concrete panels were remaining tightly in place.

Then another thunderous boom reverberated around the room—only this time, it was a little louder. Soon afterward, there were two, three, and four more. With each bomb, Peter felt the vibration beneath his feet even before he heard the blast. Though it was only a second or two in between, the anticipation of each blast absolutely terrified him.

Eventually, Erna started to cry. "It's going to be okay," Peter reassured her. But he hardly believed it himself. On the outside, he was trying as hard as he could not to show Erna how afraid he was. But on the inside, his stomach was churning, and his heart was racing. He closed his eyes tightly and began to pray to himself: *Dear Lord, please protect us! Please stop the bombings so that no one gets hurt. Have mercy on us, Lord.* Over and over he repeated these words as the bombs continued to fall around them.

Finally, after about ten minutes, the attack came to an end. No more blasting, no more rumbling, and no more shaking. Just silence—complete and utter silence. Peter couldn't remember the last time silence had been so wonderful. Soon, he and the others heard three long, drawn-out tones. It was the all-clear signal, and everyone breathed a sigh of relief.

The next morning, when Peter stopped by Herr Ziegler's house on the way back from performing his chores, he received a report on the damage that had been inflicted upon his hometown.

"The airfield was hit hard," Herr Ziegler told him. "So was part of the wall and a few buildings on the north side of town. But everything else seems to still be intact. We are damn lucky it wasn't worse."

Peter was relatively familiar with that part of Memmingen, although he hadn't spent much time there. The city, officially founded in the year 1160, was fortified for centuries by a massive brick wall around its perimeter two and a half miles in length, at varying heights, and featuring thirty-seven gates and towers. Erected during the medieval era, it once included broad moats and high bulwarks to prevent enemies from approaching the town during countless sieges as well as the Thirty Years' War of 1618–1648. Most of these entrenchments existed until the early 1800s. Slowly, some of the remaining sections of the wall began to disappear via civic expansion, with almost the entire east section being removed during construction of the railway in 1862. Now, World War II had begun to claim yet another chunk of the town's rich and proud history.

Peter's father concluded that the actual town of Memmingen had been targeted completely by accident. It was windy at the time, and all the smoke from the attack on the airfield blew over the city. So, the second row of bombers had simply dropped their load where they saw the smoke, not realizing they were targeting the wrong area.

Little did Peter know at the time, but this was just the beginning of more sleepless nights. Based on intelligence reports, the U.S. Air Force believed the town was home to a repair and assembly operation that helped sustain German aircraft production. So, a heavy concentration of strikes covered Airbase Memmingerberg over a period of three nights, destroying numerous planes, hangars, warehouses, and barracks.

Finally, on July 20, the assaults reached a pinnacle. Memmingen experienced its worst air raid to date, as the Allied forces targeted an area near the town's railway station. Forty-nine people perished in this attack.

CHAPTER 4

The Mayer family spent the long, cold winter of 1945 under a cloud of fear, anxiety, and despair. They lived in fear for their lives, as the threat of additional bombings remained a distinct possibility. They also dealt with varying degrees of anxiety, as they had had to put their lives on hold while the war played out around them. And they were suffering amid despair, for month after agonizing month, they failed to hear from their beloved son and brother, Martin.

Peter's father pursued every possible means to determine Martin's whereabouts from both the German Red Cross and the Russian Red Cross. The two organizations reached out to Martin's comrades from his company to see whether they could shed some light on his situation. Many of them had been taken prisoner at that time, and the last detail the family learned was that Martin had survived the fighting and was in the process of being transferred to a Siberian prison camp in August of 1944. But somehow, he never made it to the camp. Had he tried to escape? Was he shot and left to die by the road? No one seemed to know what had happened to him.

After months of wondering and waiting for any information regarding Martin's status, Peter's father received the following telegram from the German army:

November 28, 1944

Herr Mayer, we regret to inform you that the current status of your son, Private Martin Mayer, remains unknown. As a result, we have officially declared Private Mayer Missing in Action. No further information is available at this time.

General Staff Officer Rudolf Unterreiner

The blunt, biting news came as a shock to the entire Mayer family. For a long time, they had tried to stay optimistic about Martin's well-being. Unfortunately, this news changed everything. Many questions remained unanswered, and now, a sense of doubt and dread had permeated the household.

The telegram hit Peter's father especially hard, and he became increasingly somber and withdrawn over the ensuing weeks. Until the day he died many years later, he never stopped searching for his son; he never lost hope that Martin would eventually find his way back home, safe and sound. As a matter of fact, he added a strict provision in his will that Martin's inheritance would remain untouched for fifty years from the day he was declared missing in action so that it would be there for him upon his return. Sadly, that day never came.

Of course, the family worried about Gerhard, too. Since he continued to experience some physical limitations with the leg he had injured as a child, he did not see active combat. Instead, he drove a truck for the army. Toward the end of the war, he found himself in a rather perilous situation: he was part of a German convoy driving across the Rhine River on one bridge while a group of American tanks was traveling across another bridge at the same time. Gerhard's group tried to outmaneuver the Americans and get to safety, but to no avail. His division was taken captive and sent to Marseille, in the south of France. Since Gerhard spoke a bit of English, they made him a company clerk because he couldn't perform physical labor as a prisoner of war. Shortly after his imprisonment, survival became a daily challenge for everyone in the camp. Eventually, Gerhard was able to share his experiences in a letter to family:

January 16, 1945

Dear Father:

I hope that all is well in Memmingen. We don't receive any information about the war, so I hope and trust that you and the family are safe.

I was captured by the Americans and sent to a prison camp in Marseille. I am safe for now, but it has been extremely difficult. There were times when I wasn't sure I was going to survive.

One of my first days here, all of us prisoners were told to stand in formation at the center of the prison camp. I didn't know what to expect, for this had never happened before. Suddenly, we heard a shot ring out, and I quickly realized that we were in line to be executed! One by one, the German prisoners in line ahead of me were ordered to step forward. A guard would count down: three, two, one, fire! And another guard would shoot the prisoner dead—right in front of the entire camp. As my turn drew near, I thought for sure the end had come. I thought my life was over. Then, a miracle happened. With just two men ahead of me, one of the French officers mercifully put a stop to the shootings! I don't know why, but I was saved. Perhaps it was the Good Lord who intervened. After that, we were ordered to disperse. Those of us whose lives were spared, eight in all, have not spoken about it to this day.

Fortunately, nothing like that has happened since. But sometimes I wonder if I were better off having been shot that day. The conditions here are dreadful. During the day, we are forced to stay outside in the freezing cold. The camp is enclosed by a chain-link fence, and we all just try to huddle together along the fence line to stay warm. At night, we get to sleep inside a type of barracks, but there are no beds and no blankets. Food is scarce. We barely get enough for one meal each day.

I can't wait for the war to be over so that I can get back home to all of you. Give my best to everyone, and please pray for me that I will be there soon.

Gerhard

As heartbreaking as Gerhard's letter was to read, it did give his father a ray of hope that his son would make it home safely—especially in light of the news about Martin. However, he didn't share the details of the letter with the rest of the family in an effort to protect them from the harsh truth. He simply stated the facts: Gerhard was being held in a prison camp in France. He was alive and well, and he was looking forward to coming home soon.

Peter's cousins, Ernst and Josef, hadn't avoided military service either, as they were both taken out of high school to join the army in 1942 at seventeen years of age. Rumor had it that Hitler was running out of able-bodied men, and as a result was now pursuing younger recruits—

preferably from his Hitler Youth organization. As the brothers prepared to leave home for war, their mother made a profound request: "Boys, do not shoot anyone unless it is in self-defense. Just remember, every soldier on both sides of this war has someone waiting for him to return home—a wife or a girlfriend, a mother or a father, a son or a daughter, a brother or a sister." The twins kept their mother's gentle yet powerful message in their hearts.

When Josef went for his military physical, the doctor discovered that he had a heart murmur, most likely due to the rheumatic fever he had survived as a child. Thus, he was supposed to be sent to an armored division as a driver to keep his heart from being put under stress. Instead, on the day he reported for duty, he learned that he was to become a Gebergsjaeger (mountain ranger) and was sent to the French Alps for training. This was the most strenuous division in the army; thus, in the long run, it was probably good for Josef, as his heart ended up becoming stronger. Training in the Alps was rather difficult because all the recruits traveled on skis and had to carry heavy backpacks. Maneuvering proved to be extremely demanding and treacherous. A number of times, Josef saw other trainees slip over the edge of a cliff and fall into a ravine about a hundred feet below. Their bodies were never recovered.

The focus of the war eventually turned to the Russian front, and many men were needed for reinforcements. So, Josef was moved from the mountain ranger division to the field. He joined his new unit by train and then marched through parts of France, across Germany, into Poland, and eventually, Russia. In contrast, Ernst was serving on the Western front—as far away as possible from Josef. Every day, the twins wondered whether they would return home alive, and they prayed to the Lord for each other's protection.

After Josef's training in the French Alps and prior to his time spent in Russia, he was stationed with the army in various villages and cities in France as part of the occupying force. Friendships and bonds were formed as he and his fellow soldiers spent every moment together, often facing harsh conditions and adversity along the way. It was during this time that Josef became acquainted with someone who would become one of his closest friends, a fellow soldier named Wilhelm Albrecht, who hailed from a small town in northern Austria where his family owned a bakery.

At one point, Josef and Wilhelm's company was stationed in the city of Dijon, France. The villagers were celebrating the French National Independence holiday and invited the German soldiers along to celebrate. They ate a meal with the locals, shared a few bottles of good French wine, and even sang the French National Anthem together. That evening, all were friends—nationalities and political alliances didn't matter.

While stationed in another part of France, Josef and his company briefly occupied a small village and had the opportunity to befriend some of the citizens there. One evening, a gracious family invited Josef and several other soldiers for food and fellowship in their home. During the meal, the two sides came together to become one people.

Soon, however, the revelry ceased, and the focus of the war effort shifted to Russia.

By this time, Hitler was running out of money to fund his war machine. The most any of his troops had was but one blanket each and one wool uniform to wear, no matter the season or conditions. This posed quite a dilemma during the bitterly cold Russian winter. So each night, Josef had a decision to make: *Do I sleep on my blanket and form a buffer between me and the icy, hard ground, or do I use it to cover myself and provide some protection from the harsh elements?* Either way, the bone-chilling conditions made it difficult to get any decent rest.

As the Nazis advanced eastward, they moved so quickly that they outpaced what few supplies they had accompanying them. Suddenly, many of the troops found themselves in Western Russia, fighting both the frigid weather and the better-equipped Russians without the supplies they so desperately needed to survive. Consequently, they were ordered to retreat westward back toward Germany and their supply trains. As they did so, many of them perished at the hands of the Russian infantry pursuing them.

Fortunately, Josef's unit managed to continually outmaneuver the enemy—sometimes with a bit of help from Lady Luck. One particularly frosty night, Josef and a small group of his fellow soldiers found shelter in a barn in rural Western Russia. After some of the furry occupants caused quite a ruckus in response to the intruders, the farmer who owned the barn discovered the soldiers hiding out on his property. However, instead of reporting them to the Russian authorities, he generously offered them food and allowed them to stay in his barn.

To keep warm that night, the soldiers huddled as closely together as possible, drawing from each other's body heat. Soon, the soldier sleeping beside Josef began nudging him. After a few annoying minutes, Josef had had enough and gave him a good elbow in return. His neighbor responded with a nasally "snort!" Upon hearing this, Josef realized he had been snuggling with a pig, not one of his comrades. He sprang to his feet, snapped up his blanket, and bolted to the other side of the barn.

The next morning, the farmer offered to take the soldiers to church for Sunday Mass. He provided them with some of his own dress clothes so that they would not be recognized as soldiers, and they accompanied him and his wife to the tiny Catholic church nearby. After Mass, his wife graciously made dinner for all of them, and they shared a good, warm meal in the farmer's home. The following day, the soldiers, dressed once again in their military attire, continued their westward retreat in hopes of finding their much-needed supplies while continuing to avoid the pursuing Russians.

Unfortunately, for a while there was never enough food to nourish the soldiers; as a result, they would sometimes go without anything to eat for days on end. They would eat hard field corn or whatever they could find to get by. After a couple of weeks, mercifully, a shipment of tin cans made its way to camp. The starving men looked forward to finally having something good to eat; they were like children on Christmas morning in anticipation of presents. Much to their dismay, however, when they opened the cans, they found that the cans contained only lard. They were so hungry, though, that they ate the lard anyway and ultimately paid the price with severe bouts of diarrhea.

One Sunday, Josef's company was marching through a Russian village when they came upon a Russian Orthodox church. A notice was posted at the door: "Be our guest. Please join us on Sunday for church to receive the blessings of the heavenly Father." People were entering the church at the time, so Josef and his friend Wilhelm decided that they also wanted to attend. Upon asking whether they would be welcome, the villagers gladly accepted them, despite their German uniforms.

Interestingly, several Russian soldiers had also decided to attend the same service. During this sacred time, all were able to lay down their arms and commune as one people. Josef and Wilhelm marveled at the stunning beauty of the service. All of the men stood in the middle of the church, while the women surrounded them. The men sang lovely old Russian chants—the sound of which nearly brought Josef and Wilhelm to tears. *This music is absolutely glorious,* Josef thought to himself. This experience was a God-given moment during a very stressful time, reminding Josef and Wilhelm of the glory of God and the true meaning of life. At the end of the service, some members of the congregation cheerfully invited them to join them for a meal. Although they were famished, Josef and Wilhelm politely, and perhaps wisely, declined the invitation, for they thought it was more prudent that they quickly return to their company in light of the fact that they were surrounded by Russian soldiers.

Before Josef left for the war, he had promised Peter that he would write to him whenever he could. So, Peter longed for correspondence from his dear friend and cousin, checking the family mailbox on Sommerstrasse day after agonizing day.

At first, Josef's letters were filled with general, good-natured remarks—such as the respective pig and church service stories. Perhaps it was his way of protecting his younger cousin from the atrocities he had to endure. Peter appreciated the pleasantries but eventually wrote back to Josef asking for more.

Josef, I know you have it bad out there, Peter's letter said. *We hear stories here at home. Please share more details. I really want to know what it's like for you.*

Josef obliged with some chilling details in a later correspondence:

January 3, 1944

Dear Peter:

A lot has happened since the last time I wrote to you. I'm doing okay, but it has definitely been rough—just like you thought.

Although I haven't experienced much fighting, I always have to be prepared. One evening, I was pinned down in a foxhole by three Russian soldiers, one of whom was up in a tree shooting at me. My friend Wilhelm Albrecht called me on a radio and wanted to know how I was doing. I told him not so good! So Wilhelm left the safety of his foxhole and, along with some of his company, came to my rescue, shooting the three Russians. I owe Wilhelm my life!

Eventually, he and I were separated into two different units. One day, I felt someone tap me on my back and say, "Hey, Josef. Is that you?" I knew it was Wilhelm by the sound of his voice, but when I turned around, he was nowhere to be found. Not too long after that, my mother received a letter from Wilhelm's mother saying that he had been killed in action. I was devastated by the news. He saved my life and lost his. I couldn't help him. Now I can only wonder what our lives would have been like if we had both survived and had been able to continue our friendship.

Interestingly enough, though we don't have much to eat, we're supplied with cigarettes! So I started smoking—don't tell my mother! It's a terrible habit, but it didn't last very long. I was in a foxhole with a friend. Facing us was another foxhole filled with Russian soldiers. My friend had run out of cigarettes. He said, "I am out of cigarettes. I'm going across the line to the Russian foxhole to see if they will give me any." It was then that I realized how addictive smoking was. He was willing to risk his life for a cigarette! I told him, "Here. I have some left. You can have mine." And I haven't smoked since!

* * *

July 28, 1944

Dear Peter:

Well, as you've probably heard by now, my luck finally ran out. I was recently shot in my right wrist and left arm. It was a dark night, and it was very cold and snowing. We were in heavy combat, and we were clearly outnumbered by the Russians. The fighting was extremely intense, with many soldiers on both sides going down in battle. Others lay shot and not sure what would happen to them.

I got up and quickly moved from one end of my bunker to another, but I guess I didn't get down far enough to hide from the enemy. I thought I was safe. Then I heard this crackle of gunfire. In the blink of an eye, I went from watching the snow fall to the ground to seeing blood running down my hand—drops of dark red blood staining the bright, white snow. I must have been in shock. Since I'm right-handed, I couldn't hold a gun to protect myself, and there were no medical resources close to my unit. I had to do something, and fast! Otherwise, I might have bled to death. One of my fellow soldiers immediately tied a tourniquet on my left arm and wrapped my right hand. He saved my life. But minutes later, he, too, was shot. (I just found out that he didn't survive—I can't believe it! I lived and he died.) All I could do was lay there in the snow, waiting and praying for the fighting to stop.

A few hours later, my prayers were answered, and we were able to escape. We walked during the night to a Red Cross camp about three miles away. I thought we would never get there! We pushed ourselves to arrive before daylight out of fear that someone would see us and take more shots at us. Fortunately, we made it there safely. The doctor removed the tourniquet in time to save my arm, treated me, and then sent me on a boxcar to a hospital here in Munich for surgery. Now I'm able to recuperate and receive treatment and therapy.

One of the nurses here is actually transcribing my letter to you because I can't write with this bandaged up hand. But I wanted you and the family to know exactly what happened to me.

Do you remember that old German remedy for healing that Grossmutter used on us when we would get hurt playing in the yard? That mixture of raw eggs, red wine, and sugar? Well, believe it or not, that's what they gave me on the train ride to Munich! It sure tasted good after what I'd been through—and it made me wish I were home on Sommerstrasse. I ate as much of it as they would give me!

Yesterday, they sent me to see a hand specialist. After he examined my wounds, the doctor told me I will never recover feeling in my thumb and the first two fingers of my right hand because of nerve damage. That means no more violin! No more artwork. I can't believe it. I just can't believe it. You know I want to be a structural engineer after the war. I want to build things. Which means I have to be able to create detailed drawings of my ideas. This is my dream, and I can't let it slip away. You can bet that I will do everything I can to overcome this. I have to! Otherwise, I don't know what I will do with my life.

You'd think I'd be coming home for good after all this, but

no such luck. After I recover, I will be back again with my old unit.

It's time for me to go. I'm sure the nurse has done enough writing for one day. Hopefully next time, I can write you again myself.

> *Your cousin,*
> *Josef*

Although the news wasn't always pleasant, Peter cherished these letters, rereading them frequently. He carefully saved them—along with some of his most beloved childhood memories—in an old cigar box on the top shelf of his bedroom closet.

Peter would make every effort to occupy his mind so as not to fixate too much on the war—in particular, his relatives' plight. *They'll all be home soon,* he would say in an effort to reassure himself. *And everything will be back to normal. It has to be!* Fortunately, he had his chores, school, and the companionship of his classmates to keep him busy during the day.

His stepmother used to make bread once a week. After preparing the dough, she would carefully form it into several small, elongated loaves on a thin wooden board and then have Peter deliver them to the local bakery, which was owned by the family of one of Peter's best friends, Georg Klemm. There, Georg's father would bake the bread in his ovens. Peter would then return in a few hours to pick up the freshly baked loaves, savoring their wonderful aroma all the way home. Once, after he picked up the bread and was about to turn onto his street, he stumbled as he stepped onto the curb and accidentally dropped the board. The loaves scattered everywhere. Peter quickly picked them up, dusted them off as best he could, put them back on the board, and delivered them to Hilde. For a moment, he toyed with the idea of keeping the mishap a secret. However, he decided against being dishonest. Of course, Hilde immediately scolded him for being careless. But, with food being so scarce, she wasn't about to ditch the golden-brown delights, so the family still ate the bread that week.

Peter would spend most evenings with his sister, Erna, at the kinderler kirche (small church) a few blocks from their home, where she practiced playing the pipe organ. Young Erna worked relentlessly to master her craft, but she needed her brother to help her through the long and arduous process. While Peter couldn't read a single note or offer any particular instruction, he did provide a valuable service for his sister. You see, in order for Erna to practice, she had to rely on someone to manually pump the organ to keep it operating for hours at a time—this was Peter's responsibility. He would use a foot pedal located at the back of the organ to get the bellows going. Then, by virtue of the pumping motion, he had to maintain a certain level of pressure to keep the organ operating. He had to watch closely so that the pressure would remain within a specific range on the scale; otherwise, the organ would stop operating altogether. For his sister's sake, he willingly volunteered—at least most days.

To help pass the time during these occasions, he would read a book or study his schoolwork while pumping the organ. Occasionally, however, he got a little distracted. "Peter!" his sister would bark. That was the only reminder Peter needed to return to the proper rhythm.

Years later, Erna developed into a world-class concert

organist and professor at the Ruprecht Karl University of Heidelberg. Peter, with a twinkle in his eye, of course, always joked that her success would never have been possible without him.

Peter also yearned for his father's attention and approval, especially in his brothers' absence during the war. But sadly, because of Heinrich's status in the community as both a prominent businessman and civic leader, they rarely had the chance to spend quality time together. Of course, they labored in the yard together every so often, for Peter's father had instilled in him a strong work ethic. Peter never sat around the house and did nothing—that was unthinkable! He knew all too well that he had to stay busy; otherwise, his father would surely find something else for him to do.

As a rule, Heinrich didn't make much time for recreation, especially during the war; there were no vacations, either. However, he did own the fishing rights to a small stream on the outskirts of town. So occasionally, he and Peter would go fishing—and Peter relished each one of these opportunities.

Some evenings, Peter and his father would also pass the time by playing Sechsundsechzig. His father had all but mastered the game, coaching Peter on strategy, as he routinely won most hands.

"Why did you play that card?" he asked Peter one evening as they played. "You should have played the ten instead."

"Father, how do you know I have a ten in my hand?" Peter wondered. "Did you see my cards?"

"I don't have to see your cards to know what you have in your hand. The trick is to pay close attention to each one as it is discarded," Heinrich explained. "You must always keep track of the cards that have already been used. That way, you have a distinct advantage over your competition."

"Well, someday you're going to regret sharing all your secrets with me," Peter mused.

"Don't worry, I still have a few surprises for you," his father replied, his expression stoic.

Soon, Peter became quite the card player himself, almost to the point of obsession. Whenever he had spare time, he would pull out his deck of cards and look for a willing opponent—a friend, a neighbor, or a classmate—to accept his challenge.

He played so often that his stepmother eventually took the cards away.

"You spend entirely too much time on this nonsense!" she cried. "It's getting in the way of your schoolwork and your chores. No more cards for you."

Undeterred, Peter secretly created his own deck of cards and continued to play until he had almost completely worn out the homemade deck.

CHAPTER 5

It had been eerily quiet in Memmingen for weeks, almost to the point of normalcy. But one day in April 1945, when Peter was walking home from school with a couple of his friends, a stark reminder of the war interrupted their world once again.

"Look! What is that?" shouted Peter's friend Georg, anxiously pointing toward the sky.

"It's some kind of airplane, but I can't tell for sure," Peter responded. "There's a lot of black smoke coming from the tail."

"It's a U.S. bomber—it's spinning out of control—it looks like it might crash!" exclaimed Peter's other classmate, Wolfram.

"What are those little white spots falling from the plane?" Peter wondered. "Are those bombs?"

"I don't think so. They're falling way too slowly to be bombs," answered Wolfram.

With that, the plane went into a nosedive and smashed into the lumberyard about a mile away, bursting into flames and burning up everything in the area. Despite the distance, the boys could feel the explosion reverberating through the ground.

When their attention returned to the sky, they realized what the white spots were.

"They're parachutes!" shouted Georg. "Four of them. And look! One is headed this way. I think he may just land on your roof, Peter."

The boys watched with wonder as the soldier, an American pilot, slowly drifted beyond Peter's rooftop and landed in a nearby field. Peter, Wolfram, and Georg ran down Sommerstrasse about two blocks, turned the corner, and hid between two parked cars to get a closer look. The pilot's feet had barely touched the earth when three German soldiers converged on him, rifles drawn. A bit shaken up, the American fell to his knees and slowly raised his hands into the air. For a moment, it looked as if he might be shot on site. But after a short discussion, one of the Germans gestured with his rifle for him to get up. Then, pushing him along, the Germans began to march him to a prison camp, Stalag VII-B, located just a few blocks away.

"Let's follow them," suggested Wolfram.

"Are you crazy?" asked Peter. "What if they see us? It's too dangerous."

"Well, I'm going—with or without you two," declared Wolfram.

"Me too!" Georg agreed.

Peter knew his father wouldn't approve, but he was curious to find out what would happen to the American soldier. "Wait! Wait for me! I'm coming too!" he yelled, running to catch up with his friends.

The three boys followed a short distance behind the

soldiers as they made their way on foot to the prison camp. As they rounded a corner, the camp came into clear view. It was located on old farmland on the outskirts of town. There was a courtyard in the center of the compound, and several barracks positioned within its perimeter. The entire camp was protected by a ten-foot-high chain-link fence, complete with several rows of barbed wire along the top.

"I can't see anything. Let's get a little closer," Wolfram suggested before he unexpectedly bolted across the street. Reluctantly, Peter and Georg chased after him. Immediately, a loud crackle pierced the air, and Peter and Georg watched as Wolfram tumbled to the street.

"Get down!" Peter hissed as he yanked on Georg's arm. "Get down before we get shot, too!" They dropped to the ground, faces down.

Wolfram then sprung to his feet. "Let's get out of here!" he yelled as he ran past the other two. Georg and Peter looked at each other in amazement, then jumped up and started running after him. They didn't stop running until they had burst through the gate and reached the friendly confines of Peter's front yard.

"We thought you were shot!" a breathless Peter gasped after he and Georg caught up with Wolfram.

"They must have killed that American prisoner," Wolfram assumed. "I think the shot came from inside the camp, but I'm not sure. Either way, I didn't want to stick around to find out!"

"I'm NEVER going near that place again," proclaimed Georg. The other boys nodded in agreement.

Just then, a convoy of three jeeps sped past Peter's house toward the prison camp, each one carrying an American prisoner.

The boys looked at each other. Without saying a word, they all knew what would happen next. A few moments later, a faint but familiar crackle once again pierced the silence—once, then twice, then finally, a third time.

A few days later, on April 20, 1945—exactly nine months to the day of the air raid on Memmingen—the Allied forces struck Memmingen by air once again, heavily damaging the eastern portion of the town. This attack destroyed 15 percent of the city, killing approximately 200 people— including Georg's aunt, uncle, and three cousins—and leaving the rest of its citizens with permanent scars.

* * *

Memmingen became known as a "hospital city" as the war finally began to wind down. Because so many casualties had been sustained in the region, area hospitals couldn't accommodate all the wounded. So, the government turned the schools into hospitals and painted huge red crosses on their roofs to avoid potential attack. But instead of canceling school, much to Peter's and his fellow classmates' disappointment, makeshift classrooms were created in local restaurants around town.

The red crosses sprinkled throughout the town protected Memmingen's citizens during the day. Unfortunately, however, the enemy couldn't see the crosses after dark. During a particularly restless night, Peter climbed out of bed and stumbled down to the kitchen for a drink of water. As he made his way back upstairs in the dark, he noticed a bright orange glow outside through the hallway window.

Whatever that is, it can't be good, he thought. So, he

went down the hall to alert his father. He knocked on his parents' bedroom door but didn't wait for an answer before bursting in.

"Father! Father! There's something wrong. Come see!" he whispered, trying not to wake his mother in the process.

"What is all the commotion at this hour?" his father demanded, groggy from the unwelcome wake-up call. Peter grabbed him by the hand and pulled him out of bed.

"Look out the window," Peter replied, pointing down the hall.

"Oh, my!" whispered Peter's father, trying not to alert the entire household. "That is one serious fire, considering we can see it from this far away. I can only imagine what has happened. Is it a small town? An entire city, perhaps? Something is going up in flames. And it's not terribly far from here."

The next morning, what Peter's father had suspected was confirmed: the city of Ulm, located about thirty-six miles north of Memmingen, had been almost completely destroyed by a ground attack by the Americans. Miraculously, the only thing left standing was the main cathedral in the middle of town.

It was only a matter of time—hours, in fact—before the Americans would reach Memmingen. Since the war was virtually over, there was no sense in putting up a fight and risking the total destruction of the town. So, the mayor drove his vehicle in the direction of Ulm and stopped at the outskirts of his proud city. He parked his car, sat on the hood, and patiently waited for the American troops to arrive. As soon as he spotted the first wave of troops in the distance, he sprung to his feet, climbed on top of the roof of the car, and frantically waved a homemade white flag in surrender. Upon observing this unusual sight, a trio of American soldiers, marching alongside the first in a long line of tanks, broke into laughter as they motioned for him to come down from the vehicle and took him into custody. The mayor's unorthodox plan worked perfectly, saving Memmingen from further destruction.

That afternoon, Peter and Erna were enjoying a game of matchsticks when the room began to shake, causing Erna to bump the pile of matches and spill them across the table. "What is THAT?" Peter exclaimed.

They sprang from their chairs and rushed over to the large picture window in the living room just in time to see an American armored tank pull onto their street. Their line of sight, which was partially obstructed by the tall hedges lining the perimeter of the front yard, only revealed the turret portion of the tank. Then, in full view, the intimidating vehicle came to rest at the end of their driveway.

Uh oh, thought Peter. *This doesn't look good.*

Suddenly, the main gun barrel on the turret rotated to the left, pivoted upward, and then pointed directly at the two of them in the window.

Peter cried out to his father in the other room, "There's a big tank outside, and it's pointing a cannon right at our house!"

"Get down and get away from the window!" his father ordered from the foyer. "Hurry! They might shoot if they see movement."

Terrified, Erna and Peter immediately dropped to their hands and knees and then slowly crawled along the living room floor until they safely reached Heinrich.

Thankfully, no shots were fired. The mission was simply to protect four soldiers, armed with rifles, as they entered the yard. One kept watch over the front yard, while another went around to the back of the house. The remaining two reached the front porch and pounded on the door. Peter's father reluctantly answered while the rest of the family huddled together in the kitchen, out of sight of the front door.

The soldiers didn't bother to ask for permission as they barged inside, barking out questions in the process.

"Any guns in the house?" the first man asked.

Peter's father nodded. *No sense in hiding anything*, he thought. *That will only give them a reason to tear up the place in search of our valuables.* As much as he didn't want to, he knew it was in the family's best interest to cooperate.

"Bring them here," the soldier demanded. "All of them."

"What about cameras?" asked the other soldier.

"One moment," Heinrich told them. "I will bring everything to you."

Upon Heinrich's return, he handed them a box camera that Peter owned and another camera that had belonged to his first wife, in addition to a .22 caliber rifle and another hunting rifle that he kept in the cellar.

The soldiers glanced at the rifles, after which one of them said, "Oh no, we don't need these—just firearms." They then snatched the cameras from Heinrich, and out the door they went. Peter and his family rushed to the living room window and watched the four men congregate in the front yard for a few minutes before finally making their way back to the tank. Eventually, the tank pulled away from the driveway, rumbling down the street to the next unsuspecting neighbor's house. Finally, the Mayers were able to breathe sighs of relief.

A few hours later, however, Peter's father received

word to bring the two rifles down to City Hall anyway.

That evening, the Mayers heard another knock on their door. This time, it was Wolfgang Ziegler and his family, with many of their belongings in tow.

"Wolfgang, what happened? Is there a problem?" Heinrich asked him.

"It's the Americans. They ordered us out of our home. We have nowhere to go," replied Herr Ziegler.

"Come in! Come in! We have plenty of room," Heinrich invited him. "You can all stay here as long as you'd like."

Unfortunately, however, they couldn't stay for very long at all. Just two days later, the Americans returned to the Mayer house—only this time, they were there for a different reason. One of them pointed to his watch and barked, "Twenty minutes—out!" And just like what had happened to the Zieglers, the Mayers had but twenty minutes to leave their home, taking whatever they could physically carry or fit on their small, four-wheeled wagon.

It was March and bitterly cold outside, so the family needed a place to stay—and fast. Fortunately, Heinrich owned a building in town about three-quarters of a mile away, the Waldsänger. The building housed a restaurant on the first floor, and small living quarters were rented on both the second and third floors. The renters who lived directly above the restaurant readily agreed to vacate one of their bedrooms for the Mayer family, and the Zieglers shared a room with another family on the third floor.

The soldiers occupied the Mayer house on Sommerstrasse for three long days before finally moving on. As soon as they left the premises, Peter's family received word that they could return to the house. They eagerly packed up their few belongings and left the Waldsänger for home.

The Mayers had moved to their house on Sommerstrasse from the center of town several years prior. Heinrich suffered from a nominal upper respiratory condition, and his doctor had suggested that they relocate to the country. Not one to waste a lot of time on making decisions, Heinrich had quickly found a recently constructed home on Sommerstrasse, located just beyond the original city boundary. Building outside the town wall had become common practice in the 1880s during the era of Germany's industrial expansion. But it wasn't until the 1920s and 1930s that entire neighborhoods truly began to take root.

Although their father wasn't particularly enamored with the modern-day design and layout of the new house, Peter and his siblings thought the house was absolutely magnificent, and nothing that they could ever have imagined. From the street, the three-story home rose above the one-car garage and the six-foot-high wall around the property's perimeter. When they first moved in, Heinrich had planted shrubs inside the property line, and their height and density would grow such that they would provide an even taller and more robust barrier from the outside world. The towering house also featured a steep, triangle-shaped roof of orange clay tiles with a single chimney stack at its peak, contrasted by a gray exterior made of rough-finished plaster. Peter was especially fascinated by the number of windows the house had—fourteen graced the facade alone. The rounded corners of the house featured bay windows on both the first and second floors. Fancy dormers, each trimmed with a custom-shaped, arching gable, jutted out from all four sides of the roof, presenting a bird's eye view of the neighborhood from the third floor and attic. On a clear day, the Alps could be seen in the distance. The main entrance was situated on the right side of the house, accessible from a long, narrow stone portico with a flat roof doubling as a small sundeck that could be accessed from the second-floor hallway.

The interior of the house was equally impressive. Just past the entrance area was a small vestibule and then a double-acting glass door. Beyond this door was a tall wooden staircase leading up to the second floor, which accommodated the children's bedrooms, a changing room, and a small bath. The primary living quarters, which were located on the main level via a foyer to the left of the stairs, included a drawing room for family gatherings and meals as well as the kitchen, the bathroom, Heinrich and Hilde's bedroom, and Heinrich's study. The unfinished third floor served as a storage area, as did the basement, which was complete with a fruit cellar that Hilde used for canning.

As the Mayers walked up the driveway, approaching their house, a sense of fear and apprehension came over them. Other than a few broken windows, the house looked to be in fairly good shape on the outside. But the family knew the inside would be quite another matter, and all kinds of wild thoughts began to race through Peter's mind. *What will my room look like? Will it be a complete mess? Did I leave anything good behind? Did they take my books? My playing cards? Oh my God! Did they take...?* He was panicked.

Refusing to wait any longer, he weaved his way through the other members of his family, sprinted to the house, sprang up the steps to the porch, and saw the front door ajar. "Peter, wait!" his father yelled from behind. "Don't go in yet!"

But it was too late. Peter had already dashed through

the doorway and stopped dead in his tracks. His heart sank, and his eyes welled with tears. Soon after, his father brushed past him, took a look for himself, and let slip a few choice curse words under his breath.

Needless to say, the American troops had left a maze of destruction throughout the house. They had torn up or broken everything in sight, including furniture, dishes, and glassware. They had drunk every last drop of beer and liquor. And, as Peter's father had predicted, they had helped themselves to anything of value they could haul out the door.

This is a consequence of war. There are winners and there are losers. "To the victors go the spoils," as they say. Unfortunately, the losers usually have to pay a hefty price as a result. And that was exactly what happened here.

Peter collected himself before stumbling up the tall staircase to his second-floor bedroom. To his surprise, his bedroom door was closed, and he paused briefly to question whether he should enter. Butterflies nearly overwhelmed him as he slowly turned the handle and pushed the door open ever so slightly. He saw through the crack that his bed had been slept in, and there were several beer bottles on the floor. Then, to get it over with, he flung the door wide open.

"Oh my God," he said again. Only this time, the words came with a sense of relief. *It's not all that bad!* he thought. *It's practically just the way I left it.*

His eyes darted across the room in search of his forgotten treasure. "There it is!" he shrieked. A framed photograph lay face-down on top of his dresser, next to an empty wine bottle. He rushed over and carefully picked it up to examine it. It was his most cherished possession—a rare photograph of his birth mother knitting at the kitchen table—knitting the very outfit he would wear home from the hospital after his birth. He had accidentally left the photo behind during the mad rush a few days earlier. But it was still there, and all in one piece, thank goodness. Suddenly overwhelmed by everything that had occurred over the past several days, Peter slumped to the floor, the frame still in hand, and began to sob.

Over the next few days and weeks, the family began the arduous task of putting their home back together. Despite the damage to the house, Peter's father had foiled any attempt by the Americans to confiscate the family valuables by burying them in the yard. He did realize, however, that he would have to remain patient and alert, for there were still numerous soldiers and tanks everywhere.

Soon, additional American soldiers came to town to keep the peace until the official end of the war. To maintain a sense of order, they established a strict curfew—the townspeople could only leave their homes two hours per day: between 9:00 a.m. and 11:00 a.m. There were no exceptions—not even for work or school. So the people of Memmingen made the most of these two hours by running errands and doing their grocery shopping for the day, as there really wasn't much time for anything else.

As things slowly began to settle down, Peter received a final letter from his cousin Josef:

May 12, 1945

Dear Peter:

The war is almost over now, and I'm trying to get home to

Memmingen. If I make it, I think my first stop will be the brewery!

I know we are losing the war. It's just a matter of time, and I'm absolutely ready for it all to be over. We suffered devastating losses in Russia during this bitterly cold winter, and we weren't adequately dressed or prepared for it. I lost a lot of good friends, too. We've been through hell, and it's time to retreat. We've walked many, many miles in an attempt to reach German soil, never knowing how far behind us the Americans are.

I'm near Munich now. Most of the more experienced leaders have been killed, so they've put me in charge of a small group of young guys—newly trained teenagers—to patrol Bavaria and find where the enemy has strongholds to attack.

A few days ago, we came upon several boxcars abandoned on a railroad track. The train engine was long gone. As we approached the boxcars, we suddenly saw a few white flags being waved frantically through a small opening in one of the cars. The inhabitants were trying to tell us they were hoping for peace. When we slid the door open, we saw dozens of Jewish concentration camp prisoners. Some had already died from the incredible heat inside the cars. Others came outside raising their hands high above their heads and screaming, "Don't shoot! Please don't shoot us!"

I quickly tried to calm them down as much as I could, and assured them they would not be shot. The survivors explained that German officers had taken them from the Dachau concentration camp where they were living. When the officers realized that the American troops were not far behind, they disconnected the boxcars and left with just the engine, attempting to escape.

I could hear the rumbling of the Allied tanks growing louder in the distance. So I told the people to remain outside in the cool air near the boxcars—that American soldiers were close by and would take care of them. For our own safety, my unit and I quickly fled to avoid any confrontation.

That's all for now. I certainly hope the next time you hear from me is in person! Can't wait to see you and the family, and maybe play a game of Sechsundsechzig—just like we used to do. Take care of yourself, my friend.

-- Josef

While this letter gave Peter an immense amount of hope, it also made him extremely anxious. *Josef and the others are so close to coming home*, he thought. *What if, after all they've been through, they don't make it?* He couldn't bear thinking of this possibility. He also couldn't help but dwell on the fate of Martin. There was still no word regarding his whereabouts, and it was getting terribly late in the game.

* * *

With so many houses damaged or destroyed by the earlier bombing missions, many people didn't have a place to stay. And those who did were only allowed so many rooms in their own home for family. If a house had extra rooms, then the family was required to make those rooms available to other local families, refugees, and even soldiers. And since Peter's street was one of the nicest residential areas in town, many of the troops chose to occupy homes there. The Mayers were told they had to take in a displaced family, and this family ended up occupying the third floor of their house. And since food was scarce, everyone was expected to share what they had with others.

Peter's Onkel Friedrich hosted a German captain in his home at the time. The night before the Americans came through Memmingen, the captain had quickly slipped out of town to avoid capture. However, he had inadvertently left his uniform coat on the coat rack in the hallway of Friedrich's house. When a handful of American troops entered the house, they noticed the officer's coat hanging in plain sight, took a look at Peter's uncle, and assumed that the coat belonged to him. Of course, this was a crazy notion because of his age—Onkel Friedrich was in his mid-fifties and had already served in the German army during the First World War.

Friedrich fervently tried to explain that the coat did not belong to him, but the Americans ignored his claim. "It's cold outside. Put on the coat, ya damn Nazi, and let's go!" ordered one of the soldiers, shoving the garment into Friedrich's chest. Friedrich obliged, and much to his surprise, the coat fit him almost perfectly—which only heightened their suspicions that he was, in fact, an active member of the German infantry, and an officer at that.

Upon leaving the house, the Americans made Friedrich sit in shame on the hood of their armored reconnaissance vehicle and paraded him toward the brewery across town. There, located just behind the facility, was an open field where German prisoners from all over the area were being rounded up. Since Friedrich was the highest-ranking officer in the group by virtue of the captain's coat, the Americans appointed him commander of the German troops in custody. From there, he had to lead them in formation as they marched down to the railway station, presumably for a trip to a nearby prison camp.

The station featured a restaurant that was owned by the Mayer family brewery. When the manager of the restaurant saw Friedrich marching the troops down the street, he pointed and burst into laughter. One of the

American soldiers demanded, "What's so funny about this, you fool? Do you want to join them?"

"This old guy leading the prisoners is no captain," the manager replied. "He's the owner of the brewery. You're the fool!" Without saying a word, one of the Americans yanked Friedrich out of the formation and promptly took him to the basement of the brewery. Because of the curfew, he ordered him to stay there for the night. At 9:00 the next morning, Friedrich walked home.

Once the war officially ended, all remaining American troops moved out of Memmingen. Then, the citizens came together to clean up the town, and life slowly returned to normal—except for the economy. The Reichsmark had become extremely devalued. It had gone from a value of ten to a value of one practically overnight. As a result, the postwar years were extremely difficult for not just the Mayer family but all of Germany.

While there was still no word about Martin, the family had eagerly welcomed home Gerhard, Josef, and Ernst. Numerous other families in Memmingen, many of whom were friends of the Mayers, had lost sons. One family in town lost all five of its sons. Such tragedies were widespread—so many lives were lost for a cause most Bavarians did not even believe in.

Josef shared his homecoming adventure with Peter upon his return. At one point, he, like Gerhard, had been captured by American troops and put in a prison camp. Although he and his fellow soldiers were not mistreated, he declared to Peter, "I saw no point in being held captive since the war was basically over. One day, there was only one American soldier guarding the fenced enclosure. I told my comrades I was going to leave the camp and asked if they wanted to join me. 'Josef, you are foolish! You'll be shot!' they pleaded. But I ignored them. I found an opening low to the ground and crawled under the fence. I began walking down the dirt road, heading south toward Memmingen. The guard shouted to me, 'Hey, you! Where do you think you're going?' I replied, 'See those mountains in the distance? That is where my hometown is, and I am going home.'"

Peter leaned forward, his eyes widening in disbelief. He couldn't wait to hear what Josef would say next.

"I thought it was now or never," Josef continued. "Would he shoot me in the back? Obviously, he didn't; otherwise, I wouldn't be here talking to you right now. Instead, he left me alone, and I never looked back. I walked many, many miles to reach Memmingen. As I drew closer to town, I came upon a horse-drawn wagon. The driver of the wagon asked me my name and where I was headed. I told him, 'Josef Mayer. And I'm heading home to Memmingen.' He told me to climb on the back of the wagon and then covered me up with hay. Would you believe he actually worked for the brewery? He took me right to my front door!"

CHAPTER 6

By the spring of 1948, things had started to improve as the people of Memmingen worked diligently to rebuild their historic community. Bombed-out buildings began to disappear, and handsome new structures—carefully fashioned to blend in with existing architecture—were gradually taking their place.

Memmingen, located about seventy-five miles west of Munich, lies on the Ach River and began as a small settlement toward the end of Roman times. It developed into a free imperial town during the 1500s and ultimately became part of Bavaria at the beginning of the nineteenth century.

Peter's hometown was a fortified medieval city with several large entrances into the main section of town. The entry gate, built in 1475, was originally the sole means of access to the town during the night. Of the eight original town gates, only the Ulmer, Westertor, Lindauer, and Kempter, along with the entry gate, remained after the war. Over half of the original 2.5-mile-long wall had also survived, complete with a rather notable remnant—a cannonball left as a reminder of the nine-week siege of

1647 embedded in a section of the wall at the Lindauer gate. The moat—which had formerly served as one of the town's major defenses and prohibited enemy attacks from the East—gradually morphed into a garden adorned with various species of flowers and native grasses.

Compared to some neighboring towns, Memmingen was mostly spared, with its cobblestone streets lined with age-old houses, shops, restaurants, and businesses. It also featured a stream running through its center and a lively town square—the marktplatz—which was home to a semi-weekly farmers market and various festivals throughout the year.

Incredibly, the beloved town hall building—the seat of the town council and home to the municipal administration center—did not sustain any damage during the war. The two-toned gray Renaissance structure, built in the late 1400s, displayed a distinctive facade that included a curved gable and three turrets with deep bay windows, each topped with copper-covered French hoods and the city's coat of arms, which posed as weather vanes. The building also had a large main entrance, flanked by two smaller doors. The main gate was once large enough to allow horse-driven carts to easily pass through. Located above the heavy oak double doors was a rectangular bay with a round, automated clock amidst the tallest of the three bay window towers. In addition to the seemingly countless number of bay windows, the facade was graced with eighteen other windows and flower boxes that, depending on the season, donned breathtaking bouquets of red geraniums, giving the building an elegant and welcoming look.

Another cherished building that had escaped damage during the war was the Mayer family's church, St. Martin.

The baroque structure, the construction of which had occurred in phases between 1320 and 1501, featured a volcanic tuff chancel and a clock face on the front of an imposing octagon-shaped watch tower topped with a copper dome, and a brass weather vane cross.

Originally, Peter's family name had been Maier. When Martin Luther came into prominence in the first quarter of the sixteenth century, Memmingen became a center for the Protestant Reformation, and St. Martin Church had a significant amount of influence over the entire region. Some members of the Maier family wanted to follow Luther, while others wished to remain Catholic. At a family conference, the decision was made that those who wanted to continue as members of the Catholic Church would retain the name Maier, and those who wanted to follow Luther would change their name to Mayer.

Prior to the Reformation, St. Martin's walls had displayed colorful, painted images of biblical stories mixed with representations of various saints, and featured a total of one main and twenty-one side altars throughout its vast interior. However, the Reformation became a time of spiritual reflection by the congregation, bringing about the removal of all the altars in favor of a simple stone altar in the center of the church and a baptismal font in the shape of a chalice from the Last Supper. The congregation justified the austere look because they believed that nothing—neither colorful pictures nor ornate altars—should distract from Christ. However, the largest available wall surface did feature a painted depiction of the central Christian message of the Lord's passion, death, and resurrection. Other significant changes were made over the years, including the addition of finely carved Gothic choir stalls positioned behind the altar on either side and separated by an iron fence and gate. Additionally, an elevated baroque wooden pulpit, complete with an ornamental crown-shaped roof, was prominently displayed near the center of the church, fastened to the wall on the left side near an archway. The minister would access the pulpit from behind using a short staircase.

One of the buildings in Memmingen that had sustained particularly heavy damage during the 1945 bombings, and thus had to be almost completely rebuilt, was the "Seven-Roofed House" of 1601, the most distinctive house in the town. Located on the eastern side of Memmingen, it was originally constructed to support the tannery craft. The edifice featured an ornamental framework and a staggered series of high gables with open dormer windows to ensure adequate space for drying tanned hides. In the old days, tanners produced leather for saddles, shoes, and bridles with the help of tanning bark. The tanning process lasted up to three years.

During the war, Memmingen's annual Children's Festival was cancelled due to safety reasons and a shortage of resources. However, in 1946, prior to the Bavarian summer holidays, the festival made its long-awaited return. First held in 1571, the Children's Festival celebrates a "springtime walk" from school classes and the commendation of the best pupils of the year. The children gather together in the marktplatz to sing joyful songs. Then, a church service is held, followed by more singing, after which the children form a musical procession arranged according to grade level through the middle of town for all to enjoy. The positive atmosphere surrounding the Children's Festival's return brought happiness and a sense of routine back to

Memmingen and its people.

But nothing fueled the town's newfound optimism more than the 1948 return of Fischertag (Fishing Day).

* * *

Peter awoke to his thirteen-year-old brother, Reinhold, bouncing on his bed in a fit of excitement.

"Get up, Peter! Get up!" shouted Reinhold. "Do you hear that?"

"Hear what?" Peter moaned as he rolled over to face the wall.

"Peter! Wake up! It's the band! The band is coming right down our street. It's time for Fischertag! It's seven o'clock already. We have to go! If you don't hurry, we're going to be late."

Sure enough, a group of about a dozen musicians, complete with drums and horns, was marching down Sommerstrasse right past the Mayer house and playing a brash, festive tune intended to announce the renewal of a very special tradition in Memmingen. This was a welcoming sound, indeed, for it was the first hint of happiness and joy the townspeople had had in a long, long time.

With the exception of wartime, the Memminger Fischertag was held every year toward the end of the summer—an ancient festival believed to have started in the late 1500s. A small, trout-filled stream from nearby Benninger Ried was channeled through the middle of town to drive the mill wheels used by workers in various trades, including dyers, bakers, brewers, smiths, and more. Since the water from the stream carried all kinds of refuse and wastewater from the town, cleaning the bed of the waterway was a must. So, once a year, it needed to be drained for scrubbing and possible repair of various bridges and milling equipment. But first, something had to be done with the trout, and this led to the creation of Fischertag. On Fischertag each year, the men of the city gathered together before jumping into the stream with huge nets to catch the trout. The one who caught the largest trout was crowned the famed Fischer Koenig (Fishing King) title for the entire year.

Reinhold couldn't contain himself. After Fischertag's six-year hiatus due to the war, this was his first opportunity to actually participate in the festivities—and he wasn't about to miss them.

As his grogginess subsided, Peter realized that he had overslept and thus risked missing all the fun. Perhaps it was because he had been out late the night before, attending a party with his friends from school. He sprung from his bed, took a quick glimpse out the window, and raced to the bathroom to get ready. In a flash, he met his father and Reinhold downstairs in the foyer. Of course, Heinrich was not pleased with Peter's tardiness, showing his disapproval by pointing to his bright gold pocket watch as he turned to the door.

"Peter, aren't you going to have breakfast?" Hilde asked as she came down the hallway to see them off.

"There's no time, Mother," Peter replied, bolting outside. "We have to get to our spot!"

The "spot" was the precise location—right outside the Waldsänger restaurant—that the Mayer men had always laid claim to. Although never successful in his quest to become Fischer Koenig, Peter's father was convinced that the family's favored spot held the key to catching the biggest fish in the stream—strategically positioned just beyond the marktplatz, a small bridge nearby for easy access into the water, and a fair distance from the Schrannenplatz, where the biggest crowds gathered to hear the head fisher read aloud the maxim and blast the cannon to officially start the event. The stream in that part of town appeared from under the marktplatz and ran between two rows of businesses, flanked by a public stone walkway on either side. Gerhard had left the house at 6:00 a.m., fishing nets and stamped fishing cards in tow, to secure the charmed spot for the men of the family. Only men were allowed to participate in the fishing competition—and only natives of Memmingen.

"Where have you been?" scolded Gerhard, shaking his head at his brothers as they and their father arrived. Without waiting for an answer, he continued, "Here's your fishing card. Pin it to your hat. Otherwise, they won't let you fish. And here's your net."

He handed the cards to Peter and Reinhold and tossed the nets on the ground in front of them. Each featured a thin, wooden handle about three feet long. The netting itself was shaped like a large half-moon, approximately two feet in diameter at its widest point, with the rounded edge attached to the pole. Peter grabbed his net and moved aside as his father bent over and picked up the remaining one. He looked it over intently, gently stroking the handle with the tips of his fingers. He then turned to Reinhold and offered it to him as if it were a priceless artifact.

"This is Martin's net," he told him. "It's yours for now—until he returns. Take good care of it. Hopefully, it will bring you luck."

Reinhold slowly reached for the net, nodding in response. Despite his age, the magnitude of the gesture was not lost on him, and he radiated with joy.

Reinhold had truly made an effort to dress the part. In addition to his gray felt cap, now graced with a single fishing license on its bill, he had decorated an old green dress shirt with a hand-drawn depiction of the Memminger Mau (Moon) on the back and accessorized with a red bandana around his neck. The golden Memminger Mau character resembles a full moon and serves as the town's "charming symbol of self-derision." Hilde had given Reinhold one of her dark green aprons to wear for added protection. Reinhold also donned an older pair of trousers, socks, and shoes to complete the ensemble. The others were dressed in a similar fashion; however, Heinrich's fishing hat also featured dozens of cards from countless Fischertags gone by. Reinhold could only hope to show off such an impressive crown someday.

Erna and Hilde soon joined the rest of their family to watch and cheer them on. Having remembered that Peter had not yet eaten, Hilde had brought with her a breakfast semmel. She quietly slipped it to him and wished him luck.

Erna had an important job to do, for she was the bucket carrier—the person responsible for managing the container that would hold the fish caught by her brothers and father.

In preparation for the event to begin, Peter bent down and dipped the large metal bucket into the stream to collect some water, carefully placing it on the edge of the walkway next to Erna's feet for safekeeping. Then, turning to his younger brother, he asked, "Are you ready, Reinhold?"

"I can't believe I finally get to do this!" Reinhold exclaimed as he ducked under the metal railing protecting the perimeter of the stream. "Look at all the fish! They're huge."

"Yeah, the poor things don't know what's in store for them," said Gerhard. "It's almost eight o'clock."

"When you jump in, be sure to stand facing against the current—right next to the bridge," Peter instructed Reinhold. "The fish will swim right toward your net, and no one else can get in your way."

With that, they heard a bell ring, and the head fisher addressed the anxious crowd, reading from a piece of parchment tacked to the side of an empty wooden wine barrel. There were hundreds of men at the ready with nets in hand, lined up and down the banks of the channel as far as the eye could see. And there were numerous spectators.

"Welcome to Fischertag 1948!" With that, the crowd let out a collective roar, one that had been pent up for the past six years.

Peter bent down and whispered into his brother's ear as he made room for him at his own feet. "Reinhold, sit here on the ledge. But wait for the cannon shot before you jump in. As soon as you're in, grab your net with both hands, shove it down into the water as fast as you can, and start scooping for fish!"

"This day truly has been a long time coming," the announcer continued. "For it has been six years since the last Fischertag, and it is time for us to celebrate its return. We have spent many months rebuilding our beloved Memmingen. Although there is still much work to be done, we take this fine day to pause, reflect on our great history, and look ahead to renewing the many traditions we all cherish. On behalf of our current Fishing King, Karl Schelling, I bid all of you participants the best of luck. Let us begin. Hoy! Hoy!"

With that, the reigning Fishing King fired the cannon, and a loud boom reverberated throughout the Schrannenplatz and beyond.

The ground shook as Reinhold leaped off the edge of the walkway and down into the channel. At waist height, the water was much deeper—and the current a bit stronger—than he had anticipated. For a split second, he began to fall backwards into Peter, but he quickly regained his balance and immediately thrust his net into the stream. Within seconds, a fish became entangled in the web.

"I've got one. I've got one!" he shouted to no one in particular as he raised his net out of the water.

"Over here!" called Erna, lifting the lid of the metal container at her feet.

Reinhold fought the current as he trudged toward the bank, slipping his net under the railing. Erna grabbed the end of it and quickly released the trout into the basin.

"This is a big one, Reinhold! Excellent job!" she exclaimed.

Each of the Mayer men caught at least three trout that day, but none were as big as Reinhold's first one. As they all climbed out of the stream, Gerhard was dejected by the fact that his little brother had outdone him—on his first try, no less.

"I can't believe it. Are you sure that one belongs to Reinhold?" he asked, questioning his sister's judgment.

"Yes, she is absolutely sure!" Heinrich interjected. "At the very least, Reinhold is the Fishing King of the Mayer family this year. And it appears that Martin's net provided some exceptional help."

Peter and Gerhard each grabbed a handle on the trout-filled container and carried it to the marktplatz, the other family members following closely behind. Special scales were located in front of the Frauenkirche; here, the trout would be tagged and weighed to determine the winner. Reinhold dipped into the bucket, pulled out his trophy fish, and proudly handed it over to one of the judges.

"Young man, did you catch this big one?" asked the judge as he laid it on the scale.

"I sure did!" Reinhold proudly answered.

"Well, this is quite a sight. This is the largest trout I've seen so far at 2.72 pounds. Good luck!"

Word spread a few hours later that the winning trout belonged to Fritz Kotterer at 2.76 pounds; it was only slightly heavier than the one Reinhold had caught. Reinhold had come so close to being the first Mayer in history to win the Fischertag competition.

Although disappointed that Reinhold had fallen short of winning the Fishing King title, the family followed the long procession of revelers to the local civic center for the remaining festivities.

Amid much singing, dancing, and drinking, it is here that the reigning Fishing King has an opportunity to bid farewell to the masses. As he sits in an oversized, hand-made birch throne onstage at the front of the auditorium—complete with guards on both his right and his left—the locals honor him with speeches and folk songs. Soon, however, it's time to welcome in his successor, so the guards bestow upon him some unusual but useful parting gifts—a loaf of bread, a radish, and a glass of beer—and then boot him off his throne with a literal kick in the pants. The newly crowned Fishing King, shouldered by a group of burly attendants, is then ceremoniously carried up the main aisle and onto the stage. He proudly takes his seat on the vacated throne as an instant celebrity who will shine in the spotlight for the next twelve months.

CHAPTER 7

Soon after the war ended, Peter had to start planning for his future. About 80 percent of the children living in Memmingen attended grades one through eight in Volksschule (primary school) and then pursued a specific trade, like plumbing, baking, or construction. The others—those interested in business, medicine, or teaching, for instance—attended school through the fourth or fifth grade and then entered high school to further their education in their chosen field.

Reluctantly, Peter had moved on to high school after fifth grade because his father wanted him to become a banker, like his older brothers. However, Peter was the first to admit that he wasn't a very good student, especially when it came to language. Students were required to study two foreign languages at that time: English and Latin. Peter barely passed his English classes, and he flunked Latin—not because he wasn't smart enough, though; he simply had no interest. He never thought he would have to use languages other than German, so his heart just wasn't in them.

Peter stayed in high school until age seventeen, when he finally mustered up the nerve to tell his father that he wanted to forgo banking to follow an entirely different career path. While he knew he had no desire to work in an office, he unfortunately had no idea what he really wanted to do. He needed to come up with something that would meet both his and his father's expectations—and fast.

Eventually, the idea hit him like a two-by-four: woodworking! His brother Gerhard had told him a few stories of how, when he was a prisoner of war, some of his comrades in the prison camp would use wood from all over the world to create beautiful furniture for the American officers. This thought absolutely fascinated Peter. He excelled at drafting, painting, and other creative tasks while in school, and he had always enjoyed making things with his hands.

So, Peter worked as a cabinetmaker apprentice from 1947 to 1950. He worked all week in a professional workshop, spending a half-day at school on Wednesdays to continue his education. After he completed the apprenticeship, he worked in different shops for another three years, including Vogt Cabinet Shop in Memmingen. Vogt had a reputation for making the finest furniture in the area, as evidenced by the gold medal awarded to them at the 1893 World's Fair in Chicago for an altar they had built for a church in Kempten.

From there, Peter wished to enroll in Kaerschensteiner Gewerbe Schule, a master school in Munich. Before taking the entrance exam, however, in addition to excelling at their craft, the applicant had to prove that they had worked in highly acclaimed workshops for at least five years. This was because, as Peter would often say, "You can't learn a trade by looking in a book." Cabinetmaking is a hand-working trade, and the administrators wouldn't welcome students into their school if they didn't have the proper experience. So, Peter needed two more years of hands-on experience before he could apply.

One night, Peter ran into his old childhood friend, Georg Klemm, at a party. Georg hadn't changed much at all in the five or so years since Peter had last seen him. He still had a slight build—five feet, nine inches tall, weighing all of 150 pounds soaking wet—and a light complexion, with short, brown hair closely cropped above the ears. He and Peter made quite the pair, as Peter virtually towered over his friend whenever they were together. Peter was shocked to hear that Georg had also planned to go into the cabinetmaking trade and was also trying to figure out his next steps.

"I thought you were going to be a baker," Peter said upon hearing this news.

"Well, that's my father's dream for me," Georg replied. "He wants me to run the family business once he retires, but that could be years and years from now. Instead, all I do is clean the ovens and the shop every day, and deliver the baked goods to customers around town on my bicycle. It's not my idea of a rewarding career, I tell you! I'd rather do something more satisfying—something where I can put my creative talents to good use."

Peter nodded in agreement.

"I've always been fascinated by woodworking," Georg continued. "My mother's uncle was a cabinetmaker by trade. In his spare time, he's made some beautiful furniture for the family. I've actually been able to help him with a few projects, and I really enjoy it! That's why I've decided I want to do the same thing."

"What about your father?" Peter wondered.

"I have my mother on my side," Georg smiled. "And hopefully, one of my younger brothers will eventually take an interest in working in the bakery. That way, everyone will be happy!"

"I'm kind of in the same situation as you," Peter informed him. "My father is not too excited with my choice either. All he keeps asking me is, 'What are you going to do? You got something yet?' He'd rather I work in an office, but that's not for me."

In response, Georg blurted out, "What if we go to the United States?"

"The United States? What the hell are you talking about?" Peter asked, somewhat confused.

"Willi Henzler has an uncle in St. Louis, and he's looking for cabinetmakers," said Georg. Willi was one of their classmates. "We could go work there for a couple of years, get the experience we need, see a little bit of the world, and then come back here to the Master School."

"The United States." Peter mused. As he thought about it, he became a bit more captivated by the idea. "I have a cousin who works as an engineer in Indianapolis. I think that's near St. Louis. He loves it there. Maybe it's not a bad idea after all!"

The next morning at breakfast, Peter tried to work up the courage to say something to his father about moving to America, but Heinrich was a bit distracted. A housefly buzzed around the table while he read his morning newspaper. Clearly annoyed by the uninvited guest, Heinrich repeatedly shooed the pest away with one hand while holding onto his paper with the other. Finally, the fly landed on the table near his cup of coffee. Heinrich began to gently blow on the fly so that his wings would become paralyzed by the draft. Then, as quick as lightning, he swept it right off the table with his hand and slammed it to the floor, all in one motion. Bam! The irritating little pest would never bother them again.

Without missing a beat, Heinrich raised the newspaper back up in front of his face and, to Peter's surprise, asked, "Do you have a plan yet?"

Caught a bit off guard, Peter stammered for a second before letting it out: "Yeah, uh, yeah. I got something."

"Well, what is it?" an impatient Heinrich demanded.

Flatly, Peter replied, "I want to go to America." He held his breath as he waited for a reaction from across the table.

His father slowly lowered his newspaper, his face appearing once again. "What are you talking about?" he demanded.

Peter told him the story about seeing Georg at the party, Willi Henzler's uncle in St. Louis, and the opportunity to get the experience he needed to enter the Master School.

"Well, find out what it is, and figure it out," Heinrich said dismissively before returning to his paper.

As Peter had expected, his father wasn't taking this very seriously. He thought it was just talk, a pipe dream that would never materialize.

Fortunately, this was all the encouragement that Peter needed. He and Georg wrote to the Master School to determine whether they would accept students with two years of experience in the U.S. Within a couple of weeks, one of the administrators called them and said, "We realize that you're not going to learn anything new as a cabinetmaker in the United States, but we accept your request to work in a foreign country for two years as appropriate educational experience. Once you complete your work there, we will accept your application."

The two young men were thrilled with the news and immediately applied for work visas. Of course, this proved to be a long, drawn-out process. It would take a full year for them to receive their visas.

In the meantime, Peter continued working for Vogt and took advantage of the delay to improve his command of the English language. During the year that it took to obtain his visa, he spent most afternoons studying with his cousin, Sabine Pohl, who had offered to tutor him in English. Sabine's father, Klaus, was the president of a local language school; he spoke Russian, French, English, and Italian. Fortunately, his daughter was also proficient with languages. So, by the time he was ready to leave for America, Peter had a fairly good grasp of the English language.

* * *

As his departure for America approached, Peter spent much of his spare time carefully picking through his possessions in order to pack as efficiently as possible. After all, he would only allow himself a small duffel bag for the clothes he would need during the trip in addition to the large trunk that would carry his tools and other necessities, such as his work boots and gloves, his winter coat, and the rest of his wardrobe. He was about to begin the adventure of a lifetime, which filled him with an overwhelming range of emotions: excitement, anxiety, and even a little bit of fear for what lay ahead for him and Georg. Unbeknownst to him, however, others in his family were equally affected by his decision to leave home—especially Erna and Reinhold.

"Why do you have to leave us?" asked Reinhold as he and Erna entered Peter's bedroom suddenly, interrupting his packing.

"We don't want you to go," Erna pleaded.

As Peter turned to respond, he saw the two of them standing just inside the doorway; they were both looking down at the floor, and their eyes were welling with tears. Though they were older now—Erna was twenty and Reinhold eighteen—they still displayed an air of innocence and vulnerability that pulled at Peter's heartstrings.

"Now, don't make this harder than it has to be, you two," Peter said, sighing heavily. "You know it's just temporary. I'll only be gone for a couple of years, and I'll be back to visit before you know it. It will go by really fast. I promise."

"But why can't you just stay and do your apprentice work here?" asked Reinhold. "You don't need to go all the way to America."

"I guess you've been listening to Father, haven't you? But I get it. No one wants me to go. But it's something I need to do. I need to get away..." Peter paused briefly before changing course. "I need to get out on my own and be a little independent. What Father wants for me is not the same as what I want. I want to work with my hands, not be cooped up in some office. He still wants me to be a banker. That's for Gerhard, not me. Or even a businessman. That's you, Reinhold. I'm sure someday you will work with Father in his business. You'll be good at it. But it's not for me. And you, Erna. You have your music. You're very talented. And you're very passionate about it, right?"

His sister nodded.

"What if Father said you couldn't have your music and

you instead had to be a schoolteacher or a nurse or a housewife? You wouldn't like that, would you?"

"No, of course not," Erna agreed.

"I have to do what I think is best for me—even if that means being away from both of you for a while," Peter explained. "I know it won't be easy at times, but I think it will be worth it for me long term. I hope you can understand."

"I do. But I need you to help me practice the organ," Erna said.

"That's Reinhold's job now," Peter declared, nodding toward his brother. "He'll have to fill in for me while I'm gone."

"I just don't see how you would want to go to America, considering what they did to us during the war," Reinhold said. "They bombed our town and killed our people. They destroyed the inside of our house and stole so many of our possessions."

"Yes. They did those things, no doubt," Peter acknowledged. "But that was war. That's not what America is truly all about. That's not who the American people are. They are just like us. Ask Josef. He's been there for a few years now, and he loves it."

"I am really going to miss you," said Erna.

"Me too," Reinhold agreed.

"Give me a hug, both of you," said Peter. "It's going to be alright. Really."

The day of departure, March 1, 1953, had arrived. Peter had collected his belongings and loaded them into the trunk of Gerhard's car. The rest of his family—about a dozen family members in all, including his stepmother and father; Erna and Reinhold; Gerhard and his wife, Lotte, with their four-year-old son, Volker; and cousins Ernst and Gudrun—accompanied Peter to the train station to give him a formal send-off.

The family said their goodbyes, and Georg and his family arrived just as it was time to board the train and begin the lengthy trek to America. The first portion of the journey would be a long excursion by rail through Frankfurt, Hamburg, and part of Denmark. From there, the men would take a small boat across the channel to Gothenburg, Sweden. Finally, they would embark on a Swedish ship called the MS *Gripsholm* that would sail north to England and then to the immigration terminal in Halifax, the capital of the Canadian province of Nova Scotia, before finally making its way to New York City.

The magnificent ocean liner, 553 feet in length, was an impressive sight for the young German travelers. Constructed in England nearly thirty years earlier, the ship was the first one built for transatlantic express service as a diesel-powered motor vessel rather than a traditional steamship. It was originally used as an exchange and repatriation ship under the auspices of the International Red Cross. Now, it was about to carry precious German cargo to America for the first time.

As soon as Peter placed one foot inside the ship, he knew he was in a heap of trouble. The rumbling of the engines, coupled with the harsh aroma elicited by a potent mixture of diesel fuel and exhaust, caused Peter's head to ache, and a queasy feeling soon began to take over his stomach. And the ship wasn't even moving yet.

Once on board, an enthusiastic Georg suggested, "Let's drop off our bags and look around!"

"I don't think that's a good idea," Peter replied, struggling to speak while trying not to move his lips for fear his nausea would worsen. "I'm not feeling so good. You go."

Peter found himself bedridden for most of the voyage due to a brutal case of seasickness. He rarely left his cabin and wisely kept a trash can at his bedside during the entire trip.

Georg, on the other hand, made the most out of the trip. He spent his days trying to meet as many people as possible, and, despite the cold weather, he would often brave the elements on the top deck in order to do so.

After nearly two weeks of travel, Georg could see land in the distance. It was the morning of March 13, and the New York skyline was finally within view. He rushed down to the lower deck of the ship to share the good news with Peter. Peter barely lifted his head off the pillow long enough to acknowledge his friend before quickly succumbing once again to his overwhelming desire to stay put.

"Are you kidding me, Peter?" chided Georg in disbelief. "We're almost here. You've got to come upstairs and see for yourself. It's an amazing sight!"

In response, Peter mumbled a few unintelligible words and slowly turned over. After realizing that Peter wasn't going to budge, Georg waved dismissively and headed back out. "You're going to regret it; that's all I got to say," he called out as he made his way back down the hall.

Peter knew he was missing out on one of the biggest moments of his life. So, he eventually mustered what little energy he had in his body and willed himself out of bed. Weak from a lack of food and water, and virtually incapacitated by dizziness and nausea, he carefully weaved his way out of his cabin, down the hall, and ever so slowly up the stairs to the top deck. Once there, he found Georg and dozens of others gazing at their new homeland.

In the buzz of the crowd, Peter soon became amused by the sight of a young girl perched on top of her father's shoulders, giddy with excitement. She bounced up and down, yanking on the poor man's hair with one hand and zealously pointing at something in the distance with the other. Her father grinned as a tear rolled down his cheek—perhaps the product of both joy and pain.

Looking toward the shore, all Peter could see at first were headlights from the seemingly endless line of cars traveling during the morning rush hour. *That can't be what all the excitement is about,* he thought. Then, as his eyes wandered further along the skyline, he saw it—the unmistakable figure of Lady Liberty. He had heard about the statue from his cousin Josef, and he'd even seen a picture of it in a travel magazine back home. But never did he imagine how it would feel to see it—and its stunning portrayal of the American spirit—in person. His eyes flooded with tears.

"What a magnificent sight!" Georg exclaimed.

Because he still wasn't feeling well, Peter dared not say anything in reply for fear that something far less pleasant might come out instead. So he simply smiled and nodded in agreement.

As the ship cruised into New York Harbor, the captain's voice, booming through the loudspeaker, announced the long-awaited news: "Ladies and gentlemen, welcome to America! We will be docking at the Hudson River Pier shortly. All first- and second-class passengers, please return to your cabins and prepare to disembark the ship. All other passengers should wait for further instruction. We appreciate your cooperation."

Peter knew very little about Ellis Island—only that it

first opened as a federal immigration station in 1892 and that, over the course of sixty-plus years, some twelve million people had made it through in search of the American Dream. Since Peter and Georg were traveling as preferred passengers, they were not required to undergo a comprehensive inspection process, as the theory was that if someone could afford to purchase a first- or second-class ticket, they would not become a burden to the state. Instead, they underwent a brief inspection aboard the ship and then were simply allowed to disembark and pass through customs at the pier. Afterward, they were free to enter the United States.

Others weren't so fortunate. The experience was far different for third-class passengers, who, near the bottom of the ship, often had to endure crowded and unsanitary accommodations. And once they disembarked the vessel, they were transported to Ellis Island by ferry or barge for a thorough medical and legal inspection that sometimes lasted several hours.

Werner Krause, one of Peter's cousins who lived in nearby Binghamton, New York, had agreed to meet the young German travelers. He had moved to America about three years earlier and was working as a chemical engineer for an international camera company.

Werner's mother, Emma, and Peter's birth mother, Erna, were sisters. According to family members, Emma bore a striking resemblance to Erna. After Erna passed away, Emma had stepped up to help care for Peter until his father remarried. Thus, Peter adored his Tante Emma and had maintained a strong bond with her over the years. She held a special place in his heart because she was the closest thing to his real mother that he would ever have.

During his childhood, Peter would often ask her to tell him stories about his mother. "From the time she was just a baby, your mother was extremely headstrong," Tante Emma had once told him. "She knew what she wanted, and she never let any obstacles get in her way. I remember when she was about four years old, she had a favorite outfit that she loved to wear. It was a dress with a ladybug pattern on it. When it was time to get dressed in the morning, our mother would try to get her to wear something else—anything else—in her closet. Mother would have to chase after her before finally giving in and letting her wear that silly ladybug outfit. She was so happy when Erna eventually outgrew it."

Emma paused for a moment, perhaps a bit embarrassed, before continuing, "And, as the story goes, our mother was working in the kitchen one time when she heard me screaming for help from the other room. She came running in to see what all the commotion was. To her surprise, she found me on the floor, lying flat on my back, with your mother sitting on my chest—she was staring down at me and holding me hostage, if you will. She couldn't have been more than a year old at the time, and I was about three or so. Can you imagine? No one knows for sure how we got into that position. Every time I think about it, I shake my head and smile."

It was stories like these—and the laughter that accompanied them—that had enhanced the special bond between Peter and his Tante Emma.

"Despite her mischievous streak, your mother had a kind heart and was an extremely loyal friend. We grew very close to each other. That's why I knew, the moment she died, that I would do all I could to help take care of you."

Seeing Werner for the first time in a few years helped ease Peter's transition from Memmingen to his new life.

"Peter, I know it's been awhile since we've seen each other, but I don't remember you being so thin," observed Werner shortly after the two reunited. "You don't look so good. Is everything alright?"

"He doesn't travel so well," Georg informed him.

"Yeah, I had a difficult time on that ship," Peter acknowledged. "I couldn't really eat anything for fear of getting sick. It was a miserable trip. I am so happy to finally be on land! Hopefully, I will start feeling better real soon. Let's get out of here."

Before they could do so, though, they had to go through customs. Georg made it through the inspection process with no problem. Peter, on the other hand, experienced a bit of a scare.

Peter had built a wooden trunk into which he put a cabinet to house some of his most cherished tools. These tools represented the essence of his livelihood: nearly a dozen chisels of various shapes and sizes, several planes, a hammer, a file, some clamps, and even a hand saw, among other things. This was no makeshift carrying case. Ever the craftsman, Peter had ensured that the trunk was the perfect shape and size in order to best protect his precious cargo. He had carefully lowered the cabinet into the trunk and then neatly packed his clothes, boots, and coat on top.

As the inspector began to casually pick through Peter's clothes, he noticed that the trunk seemed to contain a second compartment. A bit suspicious, he knocked on the wooden top of the tool cabinet; and after wondering aloud "What the hell's goin' on here?" he immediately grabbed Peter by the arm and started to pull him aside to question him. Because of his thick East Coast accent, Peter couldn't understand his English very well, and he began to panic.

"Wait! They're his tools," Werner interjected. "He's a cabinetmaker. From Germany. And those are his tools for work." Much to Peter's and Werner's surprise, the inspector took Werner at his word, letting go of Peter's arm, nodding, and waving them through without even looking inside the cabinet. Werner gently pushed Peter from behind, guiding him through the line. "Keep going—before he changes his mind," he whispered.

Unfortunately, the reunion between Werner and Peter didn't last very long, as the young travelers had a tight schedule to maintain. After having dinner and a couple of beers at a local restaurant, a good night's sleep was in order so that Peter and Georg would be refreshed and ready in time to begin the next leg of their long journey to St. Louis.

Werner drove them to the bus station in the morning, and the boys boarded a Greyhound bus headed west. The next stop was Indianapolis, where Peter would be reunited with his favorite cousin, Josef Mayer. It just so happened to be March 17th—St. Patrick's Day in the United States. When they met at the bus terminal, Josef greeted them while sporting a one-dollar bill neatly tucked into the front pocket of his navy blue sport coat. Peter asked him, "What's with the money sticking out of your pocket?" and Josef replied, "It's the only thing I own that's green!"

This remark both amused and perplexed Peter, for the concept of St. Patrick's Day was completely foreign to him. "What are you talking about?" he asked, before jokingly adding, "I heard the streets here are lined with gold, but people actually wear money on their clothes, too?"

"It's St. Patrick's Day. You're supposed to wear something green. Look around. Just about everyone has something on that's green. If you're going to live here in America, you have to abide by the customs. You wear green on St. Patrick's Day—whether you are Irish or not. You wear a combination of red, white, and blue on the Fourth of July—which is Independence Day—and you always wear red and green at Christmastime. It's tradition."

"Well, I guess you're the expert, Josef. Georg, it sounds like we need to update our wardrobes!" Peter joked.

Josef had arrived in the United States about two years before Peter. After returning from military service, he had pursued his education at the University of Munich. But this didn't come without its challenges. Thanks to the war, the buildings did not have heat, and all of the books in them had been destroyed. So, the professor had stood at the front of the classroom and taught Josef and the other students all they needed to know by simply using a chalkboard and lecturing. Josef took endless notes, but sometimes his hands were so cold that he found it difficult to even hold his pencil. Despite enduring such adversity, he received an excellent education and graduated with degrees in civil and structural engineering.

Unfortunately, Josef was unable to find a job after completing his education, despite his superb credentials. Jobs were not abundant in Germany at that time, as the country's citizens were struggling simply to survive. After a long and stressful search, Josef partnered with two men from his engineering class to form a company of their own. However, the struggles continued, as the men had to fight long and hard to make the new enterprise profitable. Even though many buildings had been damaged or destroyed during the war, there was no capital to repair them—and no capital meant no work.

Josef ultimately volunteered to travel to the United States in search of new business for the company, as the U.S. was doing quite well after the war and work was plentiful. His travels led him to Indiana, and, after a short time, he came to really enjoy America. As a result, he decided to leave the partnership and remain in the United States. He landed his first job as a structural engineer for a small firm, earning one dollar per hour. A year later, he was offered a job with the State of Indiana, where his work centered on the construction of roads and bridges, and his pay was doubled to two dollars per hour. Being a good German, though, he saved half of every paycheck and often scrimped on meals and material things in order to get by.

During his employment with the State of Indiana, Josef was given the opportunity to network with several people from a highly regarded engineering firm in Indianapolis. Eventually, a position for a structural engineer opened up at the firm, and Josef jumped at the chance to apply. The firm's owner hired him at three dollars per hour. The owner became a tremendous mentor for Josef and gradually entrusted him with more and more challenging projects. Over time, Josef designed and supervised the structural plans for many of the buildings at Indiana University Bloomington, including the music school and the business school. Other major projects of his included the Indianapolis Motor Speedway, the Hoosier Dome, the Guatemalan Opera House, and the Volkswagen plant in Pennsylvania.

Upon his mentor's retirement, he promoted Josef to Chairman and CEO of the company. Under Josef's astute leadership, the firm would grow to ninety employees, primarily serving the Midwest region of the United States.

Once, during a particularly difficult day at the firm, one of Josef's employees had marveled internally at how Josef always maintained his calm, positive demeanor during even the toughest of times. Before heading out the door, he stopped by his boss' office and asked him why he never seemed bothered by problems at work.

Josef smiled gently before getting serious for a moment. "I served during World War II in the Nazi Army on the Eastern Front, fighting the Russians in brutally frigid conditions," he replied. "I was in a regiment that consisted of 950 men. Only thirty-seven of those men survived the war. I am very lucky just to be here today, and that is why I don't let everyday problems bother me."

The awestruck employee shook Josef's hand, humbly thanked him for his mentorship, and departed for home.

CHAPTER 8

Josef's early success, as well as that of Werner Krause, provided a great deal of reassurance and optimism for the fledgling immigrants. Before they left for America, Peter and Georg had pooled their resources, coming up with $200 between the two of them, and they were determined to make the best of it. Fortunately, they already had jobs lined up, so they could count on income to pay their rent and other expenses. They also knew they would be alright because they had a legitimate profession; they had learned a valuable trade back home that would serve them well in the United States.

Peter and Georg arrived in St. Louis at 4:30 p.m. on a Thursday afternoon and were already scheduled to begin work at 8:00 a.m. the very next morning. Clearly, there was no rest for the weary. Their foreman, Frank Henzler, met them at the bus station downtown and dropped them off at the YMCA on 13th and Locust Street, which is where they stayed during their first week. Mr. Henzler was also kind enough to drive them back and forth to work each day until they found a place of their own. After that, they would have to take the city bus.

When Peter and Georg went to check in at the union hall for the first time, much to their surprise, no one asked them for their credentials. This was because everyone already knew they were professionally trained; they had passed their apprenticeship tests in Germany, which is the only thing that anyone cared about. One of the bosses at the union hall had come to the U.S. from Hungary a few years earlier, so he had no doubt that the newcomers were well-qualified to work as carpenters in America.

Peter was always most comfortable in situations where he could laugh with others. And he loved to surprise unsuspecting people with jokes—the cornier, the better. So, before the Hungarian gentleman sent them on their way, Peter couldn't resist leaving him with a lighthearted story:

Two construction workers, John and Tom, have lunch together every day. John opens up his lunchbox, pulls out his sandwich, and says: "Oh geez, bologna!"

The next day, the two have lunch again together. This time, John opens his lunchbox and cries, "Would you believe it? Bologna again!"

The following day, John and Tom are having lunch yet again, and the same thing happens. "Bologna!" John complains.

Finally, Tom says, "John, you obviously don't like bologna. So why don't you ask your wife to make you something else for lunch?"

John replies, "My wife doesn't make my lunch. I do."

At this, the patient man let out a mild groan: "Have a nice day, gentlemen."

Eventually, Peter and Georg started working for a Jewish-owned company called the Guild Craftsman, owned by a man named Maier Loomstein. The shop specialized in making furniture and fixtures for small loan companies. Mr. Loomstein, an architect by trade, had designed a special fixture used in counters, desks, typewriter stands, and partitions, and it was fairly easy to build, ship, and install. Peter was responsible for making these fixtures by hand in the shop.

Unfortunately, Peter got off to a rough start at Guild Craftsman due to the measurement differences between Germany and the United States. He had worked so hard to learn English back home while waiting for his visa, but it had never crossed his mind that he would also need to become familiar with the imperial measurement system in order to do his job. So, to help make the adjustment, he found a lifesaver in the form of a wooden folding ruler at a local hardware store—one side featured the metric system, and the other featured the imperial system.

"When you work that long with the metric system back home, you know pretty well what ten centimeters or fifteen centimeters is. I have no idea what it is in inches," Peter lamented to one of his co-workers one day. While taking measurements, he would have to flip his special ruler back and forth to determine the length in inches versus centimeters. After a few days or so, the foreman saw him doing this and snatched the ruler out of his hand. He snapped it over his knee, tossed it in a woodpile, and gave Peter a new one that indicated only inches. "I don't want to see another one like this anymore!" he snarled. "You're in America, son. You'd better get with it."

Peter was shocked and dejected. Not only did he have to overcome the language barrier in his new home, but he also had to learn the language of measuring. Everything was different in America. And, because he was a carpenter, he had to deal with this obstacle all day, every day.

"I don't understand this," a frustrated Peter said to a co-worker one day. "The metric system, in a lot of ways, is so much simpler because everything is in tenths—ten millimeters is one centimeter, and one hundred centimeters is a meter. Here, it's so different; it shouldn't be so complicated. It's hard to get your brain set to the inch system, because when you grow up and work as I did over in Germany, you're used to dealing with precise millimeters on a ruler. Then, all of a sudden you have to work with inches. You might as well have Japanese numbers on that ruler. It means nothing to me."

But there was no use fighting it. If he wanted to earn a living in the U.S., he would have to make the adjustment—and fast. And so, he did. After spending time studying his ruler in the evenings, it finally began to click, and he was able to focus solely on his craft—so much so that after only a couple of weeks on the job, he had made such an impression on his boss that he was asked to accompany him on a DC-3 to Chicago to install new fixtures in a bank building downtown. This was the first time Peter had ever traveled on an airplane, and needless to say, he enjoyed it much more than sailing on the ocean. After the Chicago trip, because he was doing such outstanding work, he continued performing most of the company's new installations all over the country.

Since Peter and Georg couldn't stay at the YMCA forever, they had to find a place to live, and fast. In an effort to help, Mr. Henzler put them in touch with a German lady, Ingrid Nähring, whose husband had recently passed away. In order to make ends meet after her husband's death, she worked at a local department store as a seamstress and rented out some of the rooms in her home. So, Georg and Peter shared one of the bedrooms, and a young woman from Costa Rica stayed in another.

It took four long weeks for the trunks filled with Peter's and Georg's tools and other belongings to arrive from New York. Because they didn't have a vehicle of their own, a friend arranged for someone to drive the men and their heavy luggage from downtown to their house in South City.

"Where do you live?" asked the driver.

Peter told him, "We live near the brewery," thinking that the man would eventually ask for an address.

Instead, the driver pulled up to the Anheuser-Busch brewery, stopped the car, and said, "This is it!"

Peter and Georg looked at each other, confused. "Aren't you going to take us to the house?" Georg asked. "We're still pretty far away."

The driver responded, "No, this is the arrangement. I'm not going any farther."

Reluctantly, Peter and Georg unloaded their trunks from the car onto the street corner across from the brewery, and the car sped off. Georg reached into his pocket and pulled out a coin. "Heads or tails?" he asked Peter.

Peter looked at him in apprehension. "Tails."

"Heads," Georg stated rather emphatically, before promptly plopping himself upon his trunk. "You lose."

Poor Peter hung his head in defeat. He began walking the couple of miles to a friend's house to borrow a vehicle so they could bring home their heavy trunks with their belongings and tools.

Knowing they needed more reliable and convenient

transportation, Peter and Georg scraped up $450 to buy a 1949 Nash Ambassador from their neighbor, an old, retired police sergeant named John Sullivan. Because of his age, Mr. Sullivan really couldn't drive the car anymore; it was now simply too big for him to handle.

The boys also rented Mr. Sullivan's garage, located a few doors down the alley at the back of their house, which really came in handy during the cold winter months.

Since Georg didn't know how to operate a vehicle, he and Peter agreed that Peter would be the sole driver. Peter had never driven anything like the Ambassador before. Upon first impression, it somewhat resembled a mafia staff car by virtue of its upside-down bathtub style. Mr. Sullivan had taken good care of the vehicle, as it was in mint condition: a two-tone, gray exterior featuring a unique, jet-like hood ornament, skirted front wheels, and a sleek fastback, along with a six-cylinder engine and 115 horsepower underneath the long narrow hood, as well as accents of brass, stainless steel, and copper throughout. Peter slipped into the driver's seat and placed both hands on the wheel. A sense of pride and exuberance came over him, releasing a burst of goose-bumps over his entire body. Eyes wide, he scanned the vehicle's special features: fog lights controlled by a button under the dashboard; a powerful horn that practically screamed "get out of my way" when the driver pulled the knob to the left of the wheel; a vertical radio design, where the driver could adjust the stations up or down the dial by simply pressing a button on the floor with their left foot; and a cluster of various gauges mounted on the steering column for easy reference.

Wow! Peter thought to himself as he fired up the engine for the first time. *I can't believe I actually own my own car.*

Reinhold will be so jealous when he hears about this!

As a result of finally having a set of wheels, Peter and Georg's social lives began to improve. On the first and third Friday of every month, the German Cultural Society held a dance not too far from where they lived. It became a great way for the two of them to meet other German immigrants and to make new friends.

Peter loved to dance, and he was quite good at it too—especially the waltz and the foxtrot. So, he spent a lot of time on the dance floor. Unfortunately, Georg wasn't very interested in dancing and would typically spend most of his time hanging around at the bar with some of the other men instead.

One night, Peter noticed a pretty blonde woman sitting near the dance floor with her girlfriends. Peter could tell that she was dying for someone to ask her to dance, as she incessantly moved to the music while seated in her chair. Peter also noticed that she was regularly glancing over at him and Georg in between songs.

"See that girl over there?" Peter asked Georg, nodding in the woman's direction.

"Yeah. What about her?" Georg replied.

"She keeps looking over here. I think she's interested in you. Why don't you go over there and ask her to dance?"

"No."

"Are you kidding? She is beautiful! Go over there and ask her to dance!" Peter insisted.

"If you think she's so beautiful, then YOU ask her to dance. And leave me alone!" Georg snapped.

Peter stood up, grabbed Georg under his armpit, and began to pull him out of his seat. "C'mon, Georg. Just do it before you lose your chance."

At this, Georg sprang to his feet and pushed at Peter's chest with both hands. Peter lost his balance, collided with a nearby folding chair, and tumbled to the ground.

"I said leave me alone, you son of a bitch!" Georg bellowed. Upon realizing the commotion he had stirred, he slipped through the small crowd that had gathered and rushed out a side door.

Peter and the others in the room were stunned by Georg's behavior, for the two had never exchanged cross words before. Peter picked himself up, dusted himself off, and headed outside to find his friend.

After a quick scan of the parking lot, he saw Georg leaning up against the side of their Ambassador, puffing on a cigarette.

Peter waited a few moments, hoping for Georg to cool down just a bit, before walking slowly toward the car.

"I said leave me alone," Georg repeated upon seeing Peter approach him. This time, his tone was solemn, filled with embarrassment and regret.

"What the hell happened in there?" Peter demanded.

"I'm sorry. I guess I overreacted," replied Georg.

"You're damn right, you overreacted!" Peter exclaimed. "You made both of us look like fools. Maybe I was being a little pushy, but I had good intentions. That was a cute girl, and I could tell she was really interested in you. What's going on?"

Georg took a drag from his cigarette and looked down at his feet, taking several seconds to muster the courage to respond.

"I can't dance."

"Yeah, right," said Peter, chuckling in disbelief.

"No. I can't."

"Of course you can!" Peter insisted. "Everyone from Germany can dance! We all had to take dancing classes in school—until our feet hurt! Of course you can dance."

"You know how you hate Latin and flunked it in school?" Georg reminded him. "Well, that's me—only with dancing. I absolutely hate dancing. I used to sneak out of class so I wouldn't have to do it. That's why I never learned. And now, I'm screwed! The best way to meet girls here in America is to ask them to dance. Only I don't want to embarrass myself. You were pulling me out onto that dance floor, and it was all I could do to get the hell out of there. Sorry I made such a scene."

"It's okay," Peter reassured him. "I had no idea. I would have never done that if I'd known in the first place. Maybe we can get you some lessons. Now that you have a reason to know how to dance, it'll be worth it."

"That's easy for you to say," Georg countered. "You move around like Fred Astaire on the dance floor! You're so smooth out there—so confident. I can't even come close to doing that. Again, I would just embarrass myself. I'm not willing to take that chance."

"If you want to meet that cute girl back there, you're going to have to get her out on the dance floor," said Peter. "It's the perfect opportunity. Just you and her. Alone. Hand in hand. You can do it, and I'll help you. Hell, *I'll* teach you how to dance! And then you can thank me after you end up marrying that girl someday."

Georg smiled in response.

"We'll figure it out. Now get in the car."

Unfortunately, the dance lessons would have to wait. A few days later, and a mere nine months after they had first settled in St. Louis, the boys came home from work to find two envelopes in the mail. "Georg, this doesn't look right," Peter said to his friend. "These letters are from the government."

Peter didn't read English very well, and Georg had no understanding of it at all because in Germany, students didn't study foreign languages in grade school—only ober-schule (high school). But Georg hadn't gone to high school; he had gone straight to trade school instead. He and Peter took one look at the envelopes and decided to call their boss' wife to shed some light on the mystery.

Peter dialed the phone quickly. "Hello, Mrs. Henzler? We got something in the mail from the United States government. It looks really important!"

"It's okay, Peter. Try to read it to me nice and slow," replied Mrs. Henzler.

Peter began to carefully read the letter over the phone. "Greetings!"

Immediately, Mrs. Henzler burst into laughter and declared, "Boys, I hate to tell you, but you're both in the army now!"

Sure enough, she was absolutely right. They had been drafted into the U.S. Army and had to report to the service center south of downtown on Second and Rutger streets in just two weeks.

"Son of a bitch!" Georg blurted. "How is this possible? We've barely been here long enough to do much of anything. And now we get drafted? We're not even citizens, for Christ's sake. This can't be right."

Unfortunately, it was. Peter and Georg were required to register for the draft shortly after they arrived in St. Louis. All men in their twenties and earning a living, as opposed to going to school, had to register—whether they were U.S. citizens or not.

"This is all my father needs to hear," Peter moaned. "Just another reason for him to try to convince me to come back home."

"I'm sorry, but there's nothing you can do, boys," said Mrs. Henzler. "Hopefully, it won't be for very long."

So, army life it was. Peter and Georg packed up everything they owned, including their tools, and locked it all in the car. They then parked the car in their garage, locking it as well. They told Mr. Sullivan, "We're leaving for the army—not sure for how long—and we don't know when we can send the rent." The old man responded, "That's okay. I've got your car, so I'm not too worried about it!"

Peter and Georg were young and, for the most part, took their misfortune in stride. After all, they had had the courage to come to the U.S. in the first place, which showed that they were up for most any kind of adventure. There was risk involved in coming over, which was a consequence of the decision; however, they never in their wildest dreams thought something like this would be possible when they first decided to venture to America. They could have turned around and gone home, but if they did, they would never have been able to return.

As Peter predicted, his father was not the least bit pleased to hear that he had been drafted, and he pressed him to give it all up and come home. "It looks like I've already lost one son to war. I sure as hell don't want to lose another!" Heinrich had exclaimed upon receiving the news. Nevertheless, Peter and Georg decided to stick it out together.

The two weeks flew by, and soon it came time to leave

for basic training. Peter and Georg traveled by bus to Camp Jaffee in Fort Smith, Arkansas. They were not allowed to write home, but Peter decided to sneak a brief note to his father anyway to make sure he knew his son was okay. He penned it in the Memmingen dialect, using the old German script just to be on the safe side. *I'm not supposed to write this to you*, a defiant Peter said to his father in the letter. *But these dummies can't read it anyway, so I won't get in trouble!*

Peter and Georg attended basic training for eight exhausting weeks and had many interesting experiences along the way. One time, they were digging a latrine with several other men—a task that the other soldiers called "shithouse duty"—out where the various companies held field exercises. They were ordered to dig three deep holes to accommodate the toilets. As they were digging, they hit a huge boulder, which was not unusual in Arkansas. They used shovels, a pickaxe, and even a long iron crowbar in a hopeless effort to bust up the rock. After a few hours of painful labor and nothing to show for it but nasty blisters on their hands, the men agreed that it was ridiculous to have to go through so much work for a lousy latrine. So, they all plopped to the ground and took a break.

While they were sitting around shooting the bull, Georg noticed some unfamiliar plant life several feet away. So, he walked over to it and carefully broke off a piece.

"Peter, what is this thing?" he asked his friend.

Taking the plant from Georg, Peter replied, "I don't know. I've never seen anything like it." Then, turning to one of his other buddies, he asked, "Hey, what is this thing?"

"It's a cactus. Leave it alone!" the other man warned.

Upon hearing this, Peter and Georg realized that they

each had tiny, needle-like thorns sticking out of their fingers. As they picked at them, they started feeling the pain.

Unsympathetically, the wise guy next to him said, "Eh, you damn Dutchman, don't you know better than to touch a cactus?"

"You guys are the ones from around here," Peter answered as one of the men took the plant from him. "You should know what this is better than me. I've never seen one before!"

Despite knowing the consequences of coming into contact with a cactus, each one of the men inexplicably handled the plant and then passed it down the line for the next man to inspect. Soon, they were all picking needles out of their fingers—and cussing out Peter and Georg in the process.

A few minutes later, the men spotted the top of a white helmet coming toward them from beyond the hill. As it drew closer, they could tell it was one of the officers, so they immediately jumped to their feet and stood around the hole, trying to look busy. However, the lieutenant had already seen them all sitting down on the job, and he promptly bawled them out.

"Why are you knuckleheads out here fooling around?" he barked. "Don't you know you have a latrine to dig? This shouldn't take all day. Now get back to work—or you'll really be in deep shit when I'm done with you!"

"Sir, we haven't been messing around," Peter protested. "I work in construction for a living. I'm used to this kind of work, but I still got a blister from this. There's no use digging anymore because it's nothing but rock. It's probably not the best place for a latrine."

Peter handed the crowbar to the officer, who immediately grabbed it and jammed it at the ground. Much to his surprise, it bounced right back in the air, just missing his own chin. He then turned and, addressing Peter, said, "You, with the blister! You don't have to dig anymore; you're in charge." Then he strode away.

As soon as the white hat disappeared beyond the hill, everyone sat down again.

* * *

When Peter was ten years old, he injured his left hand in a freak accident. It was a Sunday afternoon, and no adults were home at the time. His stepmother was at her childhood home in Günzburg to visit her family while her brother, a pilot in the German Air Force, was on leave, and his father was at a restaurant having drinks with some friends. Gabi, a young lady who would help out the Mayers on occasion, happened to be over at the family garden, picking some vegetables for dinner. So, Peter was home alone with two boys from Düsseldorf, Philipp and Alex, who were staying with the family for the summer. At that time during the war, since Düsseldorf was regularly under attack, the government would send children down to the southern part of Germany to stay with various families so they could safely enjoy the summer. The first year, only Philipp came to Memmingen, but the second year, a government official asked if Alex could come too, and Peter's father agreed to host both boys. Philipp was very well behaved, but the Mayers soon discovered that Alex could, at times, be difficult to deal with.

Peter was playing with the boys in the kitchen when he got into an argument with Alex and began to chase him through the house, into the foyer, and toward the glass door leading to the vestibule. Alex ran out the door, turned around, and slammed it shut. Peter instinctively put out his hands to protect himself, but they smashed right through the glass panels—severely cutting the fingertips of his right hand and slicing open his left wrist. Immediately, Peter dropped to his knees in pain and screamed in agony. Philipp grabbed a towel from the first-floor bathroom and wrapped it tightly around Peter's wrist as Alex ran outside for help. Fortunately, he caught the attention of the family's next-door neighbor, Frau Kerner. Frau Kerner attempted to remove the blood-soaked towel only to be greeted by more blood shooting out of the wound, as the glass had severed a major vein. "Oh my God, Peter! Where does your mother keep the string?"

"In the kitchen closet," Peter told her, motioning with his head toward the back of the house.

Frau Kerner adeptly used the string to make a tourniquet in the hope of temporarily stopping the bleeding before hurrying him down to Doctor Zett's house at the end of the street. The doctor examined the wound, re-applied the tourniquet, and rushed Peter to the city hospital for treatment.

Had it not been for his neighbor's quick action, Peter might have died from blood loss, as four tendons and a major vein in his wrist had been severed. He ended up undergoing surgery to reattach the tendons and needed a full month in the hospital to recover from his injuries. Were it not for the skills of that surgeon, Peter would have likely been disabled for the rest of his life. As the years passed, various doctors told him that it was a miracle he didn't lose the use of his hand—especially considering that the accident happened in 1940, long before the evolution of modern medicine.

Peter's father immediately replaced the glass door panels with wood as a result of the accident.

While recovering from surgery, Peter would wander about the hospital out of sheer boredom, pacing the floors, visiting the garden outside, curiously watching the newborns in the nursery—whatever he could do to pass the time. His family would regularly visit him, but he often wouldn't be in his room. They would wonder, "Where did that boy go now? He's always on an adventure instead of resting in bed!"

For months thereafter, Peter went through painful physical therapy to regain the use of his left hand. His father would help him by pushing down on the hand; this would stretch out the tendons and work Peter's knuckles back into their proper place. The pain was excruciating. Peter's father would say, "This hurts me more than it hurts you," to which Peter would politely disagree. Additionally, every other day, a nurse came to the house and would massage Peter's fingers with soapy water. This went on for quite a long time. Many years later, Peter's love of woodworking also served as a sort of physical therapy and helped him improve the strength and dexterity in that hand. Without it, he may never have fully recovered the use of it.

Because of this old injury, Peter faced physical challenges during his basic training in the army. He couldn't do pushups, and he couldn't hold a rifle properly. To combat the latter problem, he was given permission from his superiors to improvise. He would first stabilize the rifle by pulling the strap tightly around his torso. Then, he would cradle it in his left arm so that he could effectively aim and fire.

And aim and fire he did! On the Known Distance (KD)

range, which was designed for training soldiers in advanced marksmanship, soldiers would shoot over a barricade at targets and then move on to a transition range to test not only their accuracy but also their reaction time and judgment. First, they would walk down a grassy aisle, then around some barricades that simulated buildings and other obstacles where the enemy, wearing a target, might spring out of nowhere, ready to attack. But sometimes, instead of encountering an enemy soldier, the target might appear in the form of a civilian stepping out into the range, and the soldier had to decide in a split second whether to discharge their weapon. Despite his physical handicap, Peter had a perfect score on the transition range and one of the highest scores on the KD range. Some of his fellow draftees would shake their heads and say, "Oh, that Nazi... that's nothing for him!"

The truth was, Peter's love of guns as a child and the many hours he had secretly played with his brother's rifle had certainly helped set him apart on the shooting range.

His shooting prowess, in addition to his German heritage, made him a target of occasional racist remarks and pranks from a handful of his fellow soldiers. Nonetheless, he took it all in stride. One time, he slipped into his cot for the night and realized that someone had short-sheeted his bed. Rather than make an ugly scene of the matter, he patiently waited until everyone fell asleep and then quietly remade his bed.

Toward the end of basic training, each soldier was required to meet with a recruiter to discuss what they wanted to do upon their deployment. And, if they had a specialty, the recruiter wanted to know about that, too. Peter told the recruiter he met with that he was proficient in German and wanted to be an interpreter or perhaps an architect. After all, his career goal was to design furniture and fixtures. Georg requested the same types of assignments.

Peter's recruiter tested him on his mastery of the German language to see whether he truly was qualified to serve as a translator. He gave him a sheet of paper filled with multiple choice questions, and Peter quickly and confidently blew through the test. Georg did just as well. After they had both completed the exercise, Peter asked Georg, "I wonder how he can tell which answer is right and which is wrong. He doesn't even know German!"

The mystery was soon solved. The recruiter brought out another piece of paper with holes scattered throughout it. He then laid it over each of the test sheets and counted up all the Xs that appeared through the holes. "Gentlemen, you both got a hundred percent," he declared. "Congratulations!"

Unfortunately, Peter and Georg didn't know at the time that they should have asked for something other than what they actually wanted to do—because they weren't given either assignment. Instead, Georg was sent to Fort Sill, Oklahoma, to work in the motor pool, of all places— ironic, since he didn't know how to drive.

Before Peter could move on to his assignment, he had to see a doctor for a physical. He wasn't sure why. All he knew was that it had something to do with the last letter of his military ID code: US55-464996C.

"What's wrong with you? What's that 'C' for?" the doctor asked him during the examination.

"I don't know; maybe it's for my hand," Peter responded.

The doctor examined his hand and barked, "How the

hell did you get in the army with one hand?"

Peter shrugged.

Wanting to know just how much strength Peter had in his hand, his doctor then said, "Here, shake my hand."

Suddenly, Peter remembered what his cousin Josef had told him some time ago: "When your nerves are in bad shape and you're doing hard, physical labor, your hands start shaking," he explained. Josef knew this all too well because of the wounds he had sustained to his arm and right hand during World War II. "So, when you shake his hand, start trembling a little bit—that way, he'll know it's bad."

Since Peter didn't want to stay in the army long term, he played along, as Josef had suggested. After the weak handshake, the doctor again asked him how he was drafted into the army in the first place.

"I don't know. They never had me do any push-ups, and they only made me work KP duty one time," Peter recalled. Sufficiently convinced, the doctor granted him a medical discharge, effectively ending his brief army career.

As the doctor finished up with Peter, Peter got to thinking, *Well, I already went through eight weeks of basic training. All I need is five more weeks in the army, and I can become a citizen. If I can make it just a little longer, I can automatically become a U.S. citizen without having to wait five years.*

"What would happen if I slapped you across the mouth and got court-martialed?" Peter joked to the doctor.

The doctor, who didn't appreciate Peter's sense of humor, sharply responded, "Jail time doesn't count toward your service time, soldier!"

Peter, grinning all the while, replied, "That's why I asked you first!"

CHAPTER 9

Peter received the medical discharge and promptly returned to his old job at Guild Craftsman, but he wanted to live closer to work. The German community was close-knit, and he heard through his barber, Heinz Vogel, about a space for rent in a rooming house in the Holly Hills neighborhood, built on a corner facing Carondelet Park. The rent was ten dollars per week.

At that time, there were many rooming houses in the St. Louis area, usually three stories high. This one, however—a stately, turn-of-the-century, 9,000-square-foot Romanesque Revival home that had been converted into a rooming house—had some history behind it. A turret, located off a bedroom on the top floor and complete with a round window seat, provided a perfect view of the park. The focal point of the house was its sweeping oak staircase, which included an oak-paneled landing lined with original stained glass windows and decorative plaster molding on the walls and ceiling. There were nine fireplaces throughout the home, including one in each of the bedrooms. Peter's fireplace featured a decorative iron screen, surrounded by yellow ceramic tile and the original wood mantle. The bathroom that Peter shared with fellow tenants on his floor contained a claw-foot tub, marble floors, and white ceramic tile. More stained glass windows provided privacy while still letting in filtered natural light. A second-floor balcony also overlooked the park and served as Peter's favorite place to unwind after a long day at work.

Mr. Vogel's uncle owned the house, and his nephew and his nephew's family lived on the first floor. On the second floor lived two women and Peter. And on the third floor lived Greta and Hermann Ruhle, as well as another tenant. The Ruhles had been married for a short time, but Hermann had been drafted into the army by then and stationed in France, so Peter didn't meet him right away. He met Greta first, and they would occasionally spend time together at the home of Hermann's old boss, Tom Richter.

Peter made other friends, too, by attending social events sponsored by the International Institute and the Kolping House. The International Institute was located in the nearby Midtown area, and Mr. Vogel suggested he go there to meet other people who had recently immigrated to St. Louis from all over the world.

One of those immigrants was Salvatore "Sam" Marino, a Sicilian who lived on The Hill—the Italian area of St. Louis. A barber by trade, Sam and his wife Josephine rented a modest frame house behind the barbershop.

Although Peter had his own barber, he became acquainted with Sam through a common interest: gardening. Peter had spent a good part of his youth maintaining the family garden during the war. So, he was intrigued by the stories that Sam would tell about his own gardening exploits, and he was excited to receive an invitation to see Sam's spread in person.

One day after work, Peter stopped by the Marino home for a visit. As he pulled up to the front of the barbershop, he couldn't imagine there being enough room for a garden on the premises. The homes up and down Shaw Avenue were built practically side by side, with just a narrow sidewalk in between. The shop was located in the front, and the house sat directly behind it, connected by a room that Sam used as an office. Sam greeted Peter at the front gate and led him down the walkway past the house.

As the narrow yet deep backyard came into view, Peter couldn't believe his eyes. Nearly every inch of ground beyond a small patio and picnic table (roughly 1,400 square feet) was spoken for—meticulously groomed as a home to what might better be described as not a garden, but a small farm. An abundance of crops ruled the land, including strawberries, carrots, tomatoes, lettuce, spinach, squash, and corn. Tucked into the corner were several fruit trees, including ones bearing figs, peaches, and even lemons—lemons the size of grapefruits.

"How the hell can you grow a lemon tree here in St. Louis?" Peter asked Sam.

"It's not easy," replied Sam with a laugh. "I have to really watch the weather and make sure the temperature stays above forty degrees. It's planted in a wooden barrel. So, in the winter, I wheel it inside and put it in the barbershop. There's enough light in there to keep it alive."

"And what about this fig tree?" asked Peter, reaching for one of the round, plum-colored fruits and holding it between two fingers. "It's planted in the ground. I bet you don't bring this one inside!"

"No, it stays out here year-round. When it gets cold, I bring out a shed that I made to protect it. The walls are actually old wooden doors I piece together around the tree; then, I wrap the whole thing real tight with tar paper. But I leave a little gap at the bottom for some airflow. When the weather breaks, I take the whole thing down and store it in the back of my garage. It works pretty good."

Several moments later, Sam gestured to Peter. "Here, take a look at this," he said. "Do you know what kind of tree this is?"

Peter squinted at a piece of fruit on one of the branches. "It looks like peaches to me. Wait, there's apricots here, too. What the hell?"

Sam chuckled at Peter's reaction. "I took an apricot tree and grafted it to my peach tree. Now I have two fruits in one."

I thought I'd seen everything. This is amazing! Peter thought to himself before showing his gratitude to Sam. "Thanks for letting me stop by to see all this. Very impressive!"

"I got some good wine in the back of the shop. Why don't you stay for dinner?" Sam suggested. "Josephine made her spaghetti and meatballs. If you like Italian food, it's the best! And fresh peach pie for dessert."

"Thanks, Sam. But I've got a long day tomorrow, so I better get going. I'll talk to you again soon."

Despite spending a lot of time with his new friends, Peter made sure to keep in touch with Georg, who ended up serving in Germany as a colonel's chauffeur for two years. Georg absolutely loved the opportunity to be stationed back home; however, it took a while for him to adjust to his assignment, as working for a colonel came with both perks and shortcomings. On the plus side, he never had to worry about being put in harm's way, and he was able to enjoy a significant amount of downtime. But, on the flip side, he didn't have a lot of driving experience, so he constantly fought with his nerves whenever he got behind the wheel—especially with the big boss on board.

Georg also had to learn how to keep quiet around the troops. The guys would constantly try to pump him for information about the colonel, especially his social life. Rumor had it that the old man loved his women like he loved his booze—salty, dark, and firm. He drank a lot, and he liked to fool around quite a bit, so Georg served as both a confidante and an escort during his numerous indiscretions.

One day, Peter received a letter in the mail and was shocked to learn that Georg had decided to move to California once he got out of the army. Even though he had wanted to become a cabinetmaker, Georg also had a passion for photography. An army buddy of his knew some people out on the West Coast who could help Georg turn his hobby into a career.

Soon, Peter would be on his own—and this time, for good.

Before leaving for California, however, Georg returned to St. Louis to collect his belongings, and he also needed to get a driver's license. Peter still had the Ambassador, and Georg wanted to use it to practice for his driving test.

"Let me drive so that when I take the test tomorrow, I'm familiar with the car," Georg told Peter. His only previous driving experience had been in the army, and the gears were quite different in a jeep compared to a car.

Reluctantly, Peter turned the keys over to Georg, but he refused to ride along with him. Instead, he hung around outside the corner drugstore to watch from a safe distance. As it happens, a police officer was standing there, too. Both men watched as Georg drove down Hampton Avenue and made a left turn onto Jamieson right in front of them. With a military vehicle, the driver had to turn the wheel only slightly to perform a ninety degree turn. Georg failed to do this properly, and the front right wheel slammed into the curb right in front of the officer.

The officer immediately headed to the vehicle to confront Georg. "Let me see your driver's license."

"I don't have one, officer. I just got out of the service, and I'm going for my license tomorrow. I'm practicing for the test."

"Well, it looks like you need a hell of a lot more practice," the officer quipped. Fortunately, he decided not to give Georg a ticket under the circumstances, but Peter had to call a tow truck due to the significant damage that the right front wheel had sustained. Needless to say, Georg had to postpone his driving test while the car was repaired at a body shop down the street. Just a few weeks later, he earned his license and left for California.

*   *   *

When Peter first moved to America, he had no desire to live there permanently. His original intention was to only stay for two years, for that is what he promised his father. He simply wanted to have the opportunity to gain additional experience before enrolling in the Master School back in Germany.

But that all began to change once he returned from basic training. He soon realized how much he loved St.

Louis, and he started contemplating what it would be like to live here permanently. He was young, and everything was still so new. He had a good job and some wonderful new friends. And he was really enjoying his newfound independence.

His desire to attend the Master School in Germany began to wane, as well. *Here in the U.S., a certificate from the Master School in Germany doesn't mean a thing*, he thought. *If I decide to stay in St. Louis long-term, there's really no incentive to go back to that school. It would be a waste of time.*

When Peter and Georg first traveled to America, they had met a German woman named Hannelore Tischner and her three boys on the ship. Georg became well-acquainted with one of the boys. The youngest was two years old, but the other two were somewhat closer in age to Peter and Georg. By coincidence, Mrs. Tischner and her sons happened to be settling in St. Louis as well, so they had all promised to keep in touch.

After the boys bought their car, they had learned that Mrs. Tischner lived just a few miles away from them. So, she would occasionally invite them over for dinner. They gladly accepted her invitations, as they relished home-cooked meals. Over time, the three of them developed a close bond, as they had something special in common: they had all immigrated to the same area of the U.S. from the same area of Germany.

Mrs. Tischner had a nephew named Harry Beck who lived approximately thirty miles south of St. Louis in a town called Cedar Hill, Missouri. Because of Mrs. Tischner's taxing work schedule as a cook in a restaurant at a department store downtown, she had little choice but to send her two-year-old son Wolfgang out to Cedar Hill so that Harry and his wife, Maria, could take care of him. They helped raise him while Mrs. Tischner worked to support her family during many long and tiresome weeks. Sundays were her only days off, and she always longed to visit her youngest son in Cedar Hill. Frequently, Peter kindly offered to drive her.

After spending some time getting to know Peter, Harry proposed a crazy idea to him: "Ya know, they're sellin' some lots out here, if you wanna move to Cedar Hill."

Although the thought had never really crossed his mind until that point, Peter somewhat liked the idea of settling in Cedar Hill. It was located out in the country; thus, it was quite peaceful, and there was very little traffic. It was a new frontier, and home to some genuine, down-to-earth, friendly, hardworking people.

Since the Cedar Hill subdivision was fairly new at that time, there were only a few houses sprinkled along each side of Harry's street. When Peter began showing some interest in moving there, Harry put him in touch with Dan Haas, the local realtor, and the building contractor, a German named Augie Lange. Mr. Haas showed Peter the plots that were available, and Peter pondered which one suited him best. He narrowed it down to two adjacent lots that happened to be located just a couple of houses down from the Becks—one was pie-shaped (120 feet by 80 feet), and the other was a more traditional rectangular shape (100 feet by 200 feet). The real estate agent told Peter that the first lot cost $750, and the other one was slightly more expensive.

"If you buy both, I'll knock fifty dollars off the second lot," the agent offered. Fifty dollars at that time was a week's wages for Peter. Although it seemed like a lot of money, he decided to buy both lots for $1,500 total. Just two and a half years after coming to America, Peter Mayer was planting some roots.

"In Germany, ground is very, very scarce, and you can't just buy it. To be able to tell my dad that I invested in some land is something he will be very proud of," Peter told Harry.

So, at the tender age of twenty-five, Peter designed his first house, took the plans to the loan officer at House Springs Bank, a Mr. Ken Weber, and applied for a $6,000 loan. He thought he might need to butter up the loan officer in order to get approved for the loan, so he broke the ice with a little joke while the man reviewed the construction plans:

A teacher asked her fourth-grade class to tell her the difference between lightning and electricity. Tommy raised his hand and answered: "You have to pay for electricity!"

Peter grinned as he delivered the punch line, his eyes squinting with pleasure. Mr. Weber, however, kept his eyes on the plans in front of him, not even acknowledging the joke. Peter gulped. Had he made a mistake with his silly remark?

A few painful minutes passed before the loan officer finally looked up at Peter and asked, "Who made these plans?"

"Well, I did. Who else would have done them?"

At this response, Mr. Weber's demeanor changed from demure to surprise. "You drew up these plans? Well then, I think you know what you're doing. I'll set up your escrow account and give you the money."

Peter breathed a long sigh of relief. However, there was a problem: he had never worked as a carpenter before—only as a cabinetmaker. How on earth was he going to build his own house? To complicate matters, houses in the U.S. were built much differently than those in Germany, so he had an awful lot to learn.

Fortunately, Peter benefitted from spending a tremendous amount of time around some of the finest carpenters in town. At the time, he happened to be part of a team responsible for building a local banking facility where he and his fellow cabinetmakers installed the fixtures and other "finish" work while the carpenters handled the rough work. The same contractor, but two different foremen, were overseeing two different crafts. So, the timing worked to Peter's advantage, as he took the opportunity to learn as much as possible about the idiosyncrasies of the carpentry profession. He would pick his co-workers' brains during lunch, searching for every last detail on, for instance, how far apart to space the two-by-fours when building a wall, and how to install doors and windows. They showed him how to create the building plan itself. And, perhaps most importantly, they helped him determine what he could do on his own and what—electrical work, for example—to leave to a professional.

Peter became acquainted with an electrician while on the job, a young man named Johnny O'Keefe who was always looking for side jobs to help his family make ends meet. Johnny's father came to America with a brother and sister in 1930 from a small farming town in County Clare, Ireland. The three immigrants were the eldest of eighteen children. Their parents struggled financially, so they sent Johnny's father and his siblings off to America in hopes that they would make a better life for themselves.

When Johnny was four years old, his father was

tragically killed in a construction accident at Lambert Field in St. Louis. He and the crew had been preparing the area to become a runway for the airport. It was noon, and all the workers had stopped for a lunch break on-site. The operator of the steam shovel decided to eat his lunch inside the cab. As he reached for his lunchbox, his foot tripped the lever that controlled the bucket, and it came crashing down on the workers below. Three men, including Johnny's father, were killed. The operator, riddled with guilt, later committed suicide.

At the time of his death, Johnny's father left behind his wife and five children. Johnny was the eldest, at only four years old. He had a brother, age three; a sister, age two; another sister, aged just one; and another brother on the way.

The O'Keefe family never truly recovered from the loss of their patriarch. Johnny's uncle, a union painter, helped out as much as he could. But Johnny had to grow up in a hurry to help support his family. By the time he was eight years old, while the other kids in his north St. Louis neighborhood played together, the industrious Johnny was constantly scrambling for ways to make a few bucks. He struck a deal with Old Man Mack, who owned the corner tavern, to collect empty beer bottles from the patrons playing corkball behind his business. He earned a penny for every bottle he turned in. Johnny also discovered that the ash pits behind a nearby apartment complex contained a treasure trove of beer and soda bottles on the weekends. So, he repaired a discarded wagon he found in one of the pits and, on Mondays after school, used it to haul the bottles to the local market for a fee. Along the way, he occasionally passed some of the neighbor kids who would mock him with shouts of "here comes the wagon boy," but Johnny would ignore the insults with a grin. *If they only knew I was making money at this—the joke's on them!* And when he got a little older, he sold newspapers at a busy street corner outside a hospital located a few miles from his home.

Now twenty years of age, Johnny was still eager to earn extra money for himself and his family. So, when Peter asked him for some help with the electrical work at the house, Johnny jumped at the chance.

Once Peter officially started the construction project, he would send the bills to the bank, and they would pay them out of the escrow account for various items such as lumber, plumbing, wiring, and brick. This is also how Peter paid Johnny and others for their help.

Of course, Peter had his challenges, being a twenty-five-year-old immigrant with little money and even less experience. But that would not deter him from his dream.

Peter had made pretty good progress on the building project over a three-month period: the foundation was poured, the four exterior walls were standing, and the ceiling joists were in their proper positions. It was now time to build the roof.

In Peter's drawing, everything looked just right. So, he set up the four jack rafters and the ridge board, resembling four huge sawhorses that would all piece together to form the roof. Then, he drove up to the top of the street and looked down on his house to verify that the roofline was the correct height. He had decided to go with a somewhat steeper roof than the norm for the area, a 6-by-12-inch pitch. That type of design would be stronger and would allow snow to melt faster and run off more easily.

Then came the moment of truth. Peter stood on the ceiling joists and labored mightily to raise one of the rafters in position by himself, bracing it with his left shoulder. He had a spike already started and his hammer at the ready.

Here she goes, he thought. *One...two...three!*

He gave the hammer a healthy swing; unfortunately, however, he just missed the nail and smashed his poor thumb instead.

"Son of a bitch!"

His bellow thundered from his lungs and echoed down the street as the rafter crashed to the joists below him. A bit dazed, Peter wasted little time climbing down to the ground, dashing to his car, and driving like a complete madman back to the city. While it took a few days for him to build up enough nerve to go back out there and try it again, he was eventually able to put the roof into place.

The neighbors would see him out there, trying to build a house by himself. "What's with that kid?" they'd say. Occasionally, someone would offer their help, but Peter rarely accepted because he didn't want to impose on anyone.

CHAPTER 10

Peter kept his promise to his father and traveled back to Germany in the summer of 1955, but only for a three-week visit.

His boss, Mr. Henzler, along with his wife and daughter, decided to make the trip with him. Mr. Henzler's daughter Bettina had never been to Germany before, so Peter wanted to show her Memmingen, his hometown. Peter also wanted to catch up with Mr. Henzler's nephew Willi. A classmate of Peter's since the first grade, Willi was the one who had originally connected Peter and his uncle a few years earlier.

The group sailed on the SS *United States* from New York City to Lea Harbour, France, and then to Paris, where they went their separate ways. Mr. Henzler rented a car in Paris and traveled with his family around France and then on to Germany. Peter took a train, first to Stuttgart, and then home to Memmingen.

Peter, of course, was looking forward to spending time with his family. However, he had another reason for making the trip back to Europe. Her name was Trudi Riegel.

Perhaps the two were destined to be together, as

Peter's birth mother, Erna, and Trudi's mother, Johanna, were close friends as young adults. They had met while attending a private finishing school in Passau, a city located in southeastern Germany near the Austrian border at the confluence of three rivers defined by their distinctive colors: the blue Danube, the green Inn, and the black Ilz. There, the young ladies learned the proper social graces of the time, as well as how to cook, sew, set a nice table, etc. Their friendship grew so strong that when Peter's father and mother were having one of their occasional disagreements— prior to having children—Erna would pack her little straw suitcase and stay for a few days with Johanna in her hometown of Ortenburg, just a few miles from Passau. As Peter's Tante Emma had concurred, Erna was totally independent and extremely outspoken. She certainly had a strong will of her own and didn't take any "nonsense," as she called it, from her husband.

After Erna's death, Peter's father made an effort to stay in touch with Johanna. The two families took turns visiting each other, and their children grew close as a result.

When Peter and Trudi first met, he was eight years old and she was ten. Trudi and her sister, Frida, had traveled to Memmingen by train for a week-long vacation. Their mother had originally planned to accompany them; however, their brother fell ill, so she remained in Ortenburg to care for him. The two sisters stayed with the Mayers at the family home, and Peter's stepmother took them on various day trips while they were in town. On this occasion, they took an adventurous hike in the mountains—Trudi, Frida, Peter, Erna, Reinhold, and the two boys from Düsseldorf who were staying with the Mayers for the summer. A passerby observed Peter's stepmother with all seven kids and marveled at the sight: "Oh, you poor lady! You certainly have your hands full." Regardless of how the sight appeared to others, the children behaved themselves and got along with each other quite well.

The relationship between the two families steadily blossomed over time. Trudi, the girl with the light brown locks, dark brown eyes, fair complexion, and warm heart, would travel to Memmingen off and on throughout the years, and Peter's Tante Emma would occasionally take him on trips to Ortenburg. Peter grew especially fond of Trudi's mother Johanna—due to her connection to his birth mother, perhaps—and even started referring to her as Tante Hanna.

Despite growing up during the war, Trudi had had a rather pleasant childhood. She was the youngest of three children to Johanna and Karl, and she adored her two siblings, Frida and Heinz. Some of her fondest memories involved the times they spent together enjoying nature. They often went hunting for wild mushrooms with their mother in the woods near their home. Trudi became adept at identifying which mushrooms were edible and which were poisonous and should be left alone. The family would also leave very early in the morning to pick berries— blueberries, and red and black raspberries—and would pack a lunch since the endeavor would take most of the day. Afterwards, Trudi and Frida would cheerfully help their mother can the berries and make delicious jellies and filling for pies and other lip-smacking desserts. Everyone performed these tasks during the war to help their families get through those trying times, and Trudi's mother was especially good at it.

The town of Ortenburg, where Trudi grew up, was

located in the foothills of the Black Forest near the Austrian border, just twelve miles west of Passau. It was established by the Counts of Ortenburg around 1120, among the most powerful landowners of the Bavarian nobility at that time. They built a royal castle on the outskirts of town soon after settling in Ortenburg. Unfortunately, however, the fortress was destroyed on two separate occasions, the result of two bloody wars in the late 1100s and early 1500s.

Ortenburg was never attacked during World War II. But toward the end of the war, the townspeople remained on high alert as they waited to see who would show up first— the Russian troops or the Americans. They feared the Russians much more than the Americans, as the former had a terrible reputation for torturing their prisoners and terrorizing the women who lived in the towns they occupied. Fortunately, the Americans arrived ahead of the Russians, and soon thereafter, life in Ortenburg returned to normal.

Trudi's father, Karl, was a miller and operated his own flour mill adjacent to the family home. He normally employed a team of four workers to help with the operation, but wartime made it difficult to maintain a full staff. As the war progressed, each of Karl's employees was drafted into the war. Tragically, all four of them were killed in action and never returned home.

So, Karl had to rely on prisoners and refugees to keep the mill going. One year, he had a Russian medical student named Alex working for him. Another time, he had a Frenchman help out. Neither of these young men could communicate very well because of the language barrier, but they provided tremendous support for Karl. They were held captive at a local prison camp. Each morning, a German soldier dropped them off at the mill, and in the evening, the soldier would pick them up again and drive them back to the camp. Many prisoners at that time were required to help out on farms and in other industries because a significant portion of the German workforce was serving in the war. More than five million civilian workers and nearly two million prisoners of war were eventually brought to Germany to work in key industries and on the land. Many died from poor living conditions, mistreatment, and malnutrition. However, Karl did all that he could to take care of those who helped him at his mill, often sharing with them what little food the family had to spare.

Trudi had a special friend who worked as a regular employee in the mill during the week: a delightful young man named Erich. Erich would go home to his family farm on Sundays, and sometimes would take Trudi with him on his bicycle. Trudi adored Erich, who was several years older than her. She thought of him as an older brother and mentor. Sadly, Erich lost his promising life in the war, too.

When the war came to a merciful end, Trudi was eager to put the entire experience behind her and see what the future held. But little did she know, her life was about to change forever.

One autumn day during the dinner hour, Trudi noticed that her father hadn't come home from the mill yet. This was rather unusual, for he always made it to the table on time—even on particularly long, hard days on the job.

"Your father is not here yet?" a surprised Johanna asked Trudi as she brought a plate of wurst and cheese to the table. "It's dinner time. Why is he so late?"

"He is probably busy and just lost track of the time. I will get him," Trudi happily volunteered.

Karl and Trudi had a special bond. Trudi loved her father dearly, and often worried about his health and well-being. He suffered from a severe digestive problem that limited the amount of food he could eat at any one time, the result of having been victimized by a poisonous gas assault at the hands of the British during World War I. Since the family came from modest means and food was rather scarce, at mealtimes, Johanna would save the finest helpings for Karl so that he could maintain his strength throughout the workday. However, he often had difficulties finishing his meal and would regularly sneak leftovers to his devoted daughter, who always sat by his side at the dinner table.

Trudi hurried out the back door of the house and down the path to the mill just beyond the family garden. It was dusk, but she couldn't see any light shining through the building's open window.

That's odd, she thought. *If he's not in there, where in the world could he be?*

Instead of turning around to go back to the house, she decided to check inside just to be sure. She used both hands to slide open the heavy wooden door and fumbled for the light switch on the wall to her left. "Father, are you here? Father?"

With a flick of the switch, just enough soft light filled the vast space inside to reveal Trudi's worst nightmare. First, she saw a crumpled sack of flour on the ground next to the milling equipment located in the middle of the workshop. Then, the unthinkable: her father's lifeless body lying in a large pool of blood that had accumulated on the oak floor underneath his head. It appeared that he had fallen while trying to carry the one-hundred-pound bag and gashed his head on a sharp edge of the flour sacking machine.

For a moment, Trudi stood paralyzed at the door, not knowing for sure if what she was seeing was actually real. Was she dreaming, perhaps? Or was this some type of cruel joke? Ultimately, the reality of the scene overwhelmed her, and she let out a frantic, piercing scream. She raced back out the door, still screaming, but she couldn't get away from the ghastly sight fast enough. She tripped on some brick edging along the dirt path halfway to the house and tumbled face-first to the ground. The screams continued internally, but no audible sound came from her lips, as huge, deep sobs were beginning to overtake her ability to make noise. She began to hyperventilate. Unable to catch her breath, she rolled over onto her back. A few seconds later, she heard her brother's voice.

"Trudi! Trudi!" he shouted as he ran to her. When he finally reached her, he knelt down and tried to help her up. "We could hear your screams all the way up at the house. What happened? Are you alright?"

Gasping for breath, Trudi sat up and struggled to utter a word—any word. "Fa...Father," she whispered, mustering enough composure to point toward the mill.

Heinz slowly rose, not sure what to think. Then, as he turned and faced the mill, he suddenly realized what had prompted Trudi to scream. No, it wasn't the fact that she had tripped and fallen to the ground, as he had originally thought. There, through the large, dimly lit doorway on the side of the building, he could see the disturbing image himself.

"Father!" he shouted, as he raced toward the mill. But it was too late.

Karl, a quiet, gentle soul, had long borne the burden of numerous physical and emotional ailments. In addition to his acute digestive problem, he had developed a painful arthritic condition that had made it increasingly difficult for him to handle the physical demands of his job. Despite being in his mid-fifties, he had grown weak and frail over the years. Perhaps his heart gave out. Or, maybe, it was simply a tragic accident. No one knew for sure, and the family was left with plenty of unanswered questions and tears.

The next few days were especially difficult for Trudi and her family. Almost immediately, friends and neighbors offered their love and support, bringing home-cooked meals, flowers, and condolences. Each time someone new came to the door, the emotions and heartache would pour out again from within poor Trudi as she relived her father's untimely death in her mind.

The day of the funeral service—and perhaps, the family's closure—arrived. Mourners packed the church, the women sitting in the pews to the left, and the men to the right. The minister delivered an uplifting and heartfelt eulogy, but Trudi, still numb, barely heard a word of it. At the conclusion of the graveside service, each female received a red rose to toss on top of the modest coffin as it was being lowered into the ground. Trudi chose to keep hers as a vestige to her father, instead. She dried it out in her room over the next several days, carefully hanging it upside down by a piece of string. Once it was adequately preserved, she pressed it in her bible on the page of her favorite passage, Psalm 27: "The Lord is my light and my salvation; whom should I fear? The Lord is my life's refuge; of whom should I be afraid?"

Trudi had lost her beloved father. Now, at barely twenty years old, she needed some time to figure out what to do next. She had always been fascinated by animals, plants, and the outdoors. So instead of going to finishing school right away, she attended "school" on a farm that emphasized gardening. Upon completion of her studies over a six-month period, she transferred to a finishing school, following in her mother's and sister's footsteps.

When Peter left Germany for the U.S. in 1953, Trudi traveled to Enfield, England—a small town located just outside of London. There, she spent nearly two years working in a local household, doing some housecleaning and cooking for a young couple who did not have children. They were extremely nice people who treated Trudi very well, and she thoroughly enjoyed her time there. As a bonus, the coronation of Queen Elizabeth took place during Trudi's stay, so it was a fascinating time to be living in England.

Peter and Trudi, while they had never dated, remained good friends over the years and would often exchange letters to keep in touch.

June 14, 1953

Dear Peter:

Thank you so much for the candy you sent with your last letter. What a pleasant surprise! I was especially touched by the beautiful wooden box you made for it. Mr. and Mrs. Lewis were equally impressed by your work.

It has been such an exciting time here. As you know, Elizabeth II was crowned the Queen of England a couple of weeks ago, and I had an opportunity to witness some of the events.

Mr. Lewis has a colleague who provided us tickets to one of the festivals, and we also attended the parade where hundreds of thousands of people lined the streets in hopes of getting a glimpse of the new queen. The procession began at the palace, led by royal guards riding a team of white horses that were pulling a gilded coach carrying the queen and her husband Philip. We were waiting with a large group near Westminster Abbey, and suddenly we heard this incredible roar from the crowd. The carriage turned the corner, and there she was, in her sparkling crown, wearing a lovely white, lace gown and gloves, with a huge bouquet of white roses on her lap. She looked out her window and waved right at us! It was quite an amazing moment!

Once the queen left our sight, Mr. Lewis and his colleague quickly escorted us through the crowd and down the street to a private party in a hotel a few blocks away, where we were able to watch the coronation on live television.

To succeed her father, King George VI, after his death must have been extremely difficult for her. What an enormous job for such a young woman—to be the reigning monarch of her country at just 27 years of age. I find it hard to believe that she is only two years older than me! Maybe someday I can become a queen, too!

Now it is back to reality, although I thoroughly enjoy working for Mr. and Mrs. Lewis. They keep me busy with the household chores, but they also grant me a lot of free time to do some sightseeing around London. So far, I've had the opportunity to tour the National Gallery, the Tower of London, and my favorite, Kensington Gardens. Now that the coronation festivities are complete, I hope to visit Buckingham Palace in a few weeks.

Peter, I hope all is well with you and Georg. According to your letter, it sounds like the two of you are beginning to adjust to life in America. Thank you again for the thoughtful gift. I look forward to hearing back from you soon.

Yours truly,
Trudi

Trudi eventually returned to Germany for good and landed a secretarial job at the Botanical Garden in Munich. Peter came to visit her upon his return to Germany. The two of them spent three wonderful days together touring Munich before traveling to see Trudi's sister, Frida, who was now married and living in Austria. They also took Trudi's mother along for the visit.

It was there that Peter was going to make the second-most important decision of his life: he was going to ask Trudi to marry him. This was something he had been contemplating for several weeks. He didn't have a ring, but that didn't matter. He wanted to seize the moment while he had the chance.

At sunset that evening, the couple sat alone on a small wooden bench in the colorful flower garden behind Frida's house, complete with blue creeping phlox, pink hydrangeas, purple avens, and yellow gentians. It was a very quaint, romantic setting.

Gazing at Trudi, her short brown hair shimmering in the dusk light, Peter thought to himself, *Wow, she is more beautiful than I even remembered.* Then, trying to maintain his courage, he looked down and reached for her hand.

"Trudi, would you like to get married and move to the United States?" he asked her in a single breath.

Before she could respond, Peter quickly added, "I know this is fast—we've only been together for a short time—but it's been great spending these last few days with you. And we've known each other practically our whole lives. I know we can make a good life together. I know it's right."

Trudi gently squeezed his hand and responded, "Yes, Peter, I will marry you."

Peter smiled, hugged her for a few seconds, and then whispered in her ear, "Even if you have to move?" He had to ask just to be sure.

Trudi let go, looked him in the eyes, and nodded. "Even if I have to move," she replied, without hesitation. "I've lived in England. I know the language. And I know you love it there, so I have no doubt I will, too."

A rush of different emotions—relief, excitement, pure joy, and even a little fear—swept over Peter.

Soon they went inside and broke the news to the family. Everyone was shocked and thrilled at the same time.

"Were you two planning this for a while?" Frida asked Trudi later when the two of them were alone in the kitchen preparing dinner.

"No."

"So you were really surprised?"

"No, not really," Trudi answered. "When he suggested that we take Mother and come visit you, I kind of had a feeling something like this was going to happen."

"I'm really happy for you," said Frida. "But I don't want to see you move so far away."

"I know," Trudi said. "But it won't be forever. I'm sure we'll only be over there for two or maybe three years, and then we'll be back. Especially once we have children. Peter's father wants him back home eventually. So I'm sure it will just be a matter of time."

From there, the newly engaged couple traveled to Memmingen to share the good news with Peter's family. The first evening that they were home, Peter pulled his father aside and asked if he could help him find the right engagement ring for Trudi.

"We have to go to Honacker," Heinrich responded. "That's where I went for your mother's ring. He will take care of you. He does great work." After pausing for a moment, he also took the opportunity to prod Peter into moving back to Germany. "You're getting married," he reminded him. "Trudi is not going to be content with living so far away from her family. Now is the time to come home. You have enough training for Master School. There is no need to stay in America. This is where you both belong—right here in Memmingen."

"Father, I love living in St. Louis," Peter protested. "I've made so many friends there. Josef is nearby. The job is going well. I've been doing a lot of thinking about it, and I'm not ready to give it all up. I'm not sure if I'll ever want to give it up. You know I bought that land. I've started to build a house on it."

Heinrich rubbed the top of his balding head with his right hand and scowled. It was an all-too-familiar look Peter remembered so vividly as a child. Piercing blue eyes. Furrowed brow. It sent a shiver down his spine. *Oh my*, he thought to himself. *I haven't missed this at all!*

"Well, what does Trudi think about this?" his father snapped.

"She will be fine," Peter answered simply.

They were then interrupted by the sound of church bells in the distance. *Whew!* Peter thought to himself before murmuring, "I need to get Trudi for dinner." He turned away from his father, not daring to look back.

CHAPTER 11

It would take a year for Trudi to receive her visa. In the meantime, Peter returned to St. Louis, and Trudi stayed in Munich until it was time to get married. They kept in touch via written correspondence—phone calls were a rarity due to the expense. Trudi would talk about the wedding plans and her job at the garden, and Peter would give her updates on how the construction of the new house was coming along.

After several months of separation and preparation, the big day finally arrived: September 15, 1956. While a light rain fell throughout the day, it didn't put a damper on the festivities. German tradition requires that the couple participate in two separate ceremonies: a civil ceremony, which is legally binding, and a church service. The brief civil ceremony took place during the morning at City Hall in Memmingen, where Peter's father and Trudi's brother-in-law, Rolf, served as the witnesses. No other family members were present—again, this was the custom.

The church service occurred later that afternoon at St. Martin's. Peter stood in front of the altar as he waited for

Trudi to make her entrance. A bit overwhelmed by the moment, he thought he might pass out from nerves, as his heart had begun to beat rapidly, and beads of sweat were forming above his upper lip. He pulled out a handkerchief from his pocket and began to lightly dab his face, scanning the crowd in hopes that no one would notice his distress. Then, he gazed up at the choir loft in the back of the church and received a reassuring nod from his sister, Erna. For an instant, Peter thought back to the countless hours he had spent with her during organ practice. Now, on the most important day of his life, the notes she delivered from her immensely talented fingers had never sounded more glorious, and they comforted him during his time of need.

Calmness enveloped Peter—that is, until he caught sight of his new bride being escorted up the long aisle by her brother Heinz. *My goodness; how beautiful she looks!* he marveled. Once again, butterflies filled his gut—only this time, they were the good kind. His eyes glistened, and a huge smile spread across his face as Trudi and Heinz reached him.

Hours later, Peter's smile still hadn't left his face as the couple celebrated with family and many friends at a reception in their honor. The party was held at one of the premier hotels in all of Memmingen, the Adler, and was complete with plenty of delicious food, live music, and lots of dancing.

Peter's father, donning a black top hat, tails, and a cane, delivered a heartfelt toast to the young couple, also taking the opportunity to inject a little humor into his remarks. "I'm afraid I have some bad news to share with the two of you. The United States government just announced that they are revoking all visas until further notice. It looks like you will have to stay here in Germany after all!" He paused for effect, then let out a chuckle and reassured them it was merely a joke.

The newlyweds stayed at the Adler that first night, but they didn't take an official honeymoon. Instead, they enjoyed a couple of relaxing days in Memmingen before renting a Volkswagen convertible and doing some traveling—first to Ortenburg and Austria to spend time with Trudi's family, and then to Lake Constance. They left for the U.S. about two weeks later. Scenic Lake Constance, the third-largest freshwater lake in Europe, is located where Germany, Austria, and Switzerland meet and covers just over 200 square miles. It is fed by the Rhine River and features ten islands, including Mainau, which is home to a wonderful botanical garden and wildlife reserve that Peter knew Trudi would especially enjoy.

Upon their return to Memmingen, the couple used the remainder of their time to prepare for their voyage to America. Just as he had done three years earlier for himself, Peter made a wooden crate and packed all of Trudi's belongings for the long trip across the Atlantic. He also shipped his coveted workbench—a Christmas gift he had received from his father a few years earlier.

From the moment she said yes to Peter's proposal, Trudi knew she would have to move to America to start a new life with him. She was fairly young and, admittedly, a little naive. But she was extremely excited about the adventures that lied ahead.

Not knowing how long it would take before they would see their sister again, Frida and Heinz accompanied the newlyweds on the train ride from Munich to Belgium. Once there, Peter and Trudi were set to board the MS *Maasdam*, which would take them to New York.

"I don't want you to go," Frida playfully whined as she hugged Trudi with all her might, tears starting to roll down both her rosy cheeks. "With me living in Austria, we don't see each other enough as it is. How will we manage with you so far away now?"

"It's going to be alright," Trudi reassured her. "Really. I promise to write every week. And I'll be back here for a visit before you know it." Then, turning to Heinz, she added, "In the meantime, Heinz, please take good care of Mother." Heinz lived in Passau, roughly twenty minutes from their mother and the family home in Ortenburg.

"You have nothing to worry about," Heinz said, fighting back tears of his own. "Now get on that ship—before Frida runs away with your suitcase!" His quick wit made everyone burst into laughter, allowing them to briefly forget their sadness.

"It's time to go, Trudi," Peter whispered as he gently touched his wife's shoulder. "Goodbye, Frida. Heinz."

And then they were gone.

Of course, Peter was not looking forward to another long journey aboard a ship. Needless to say, he was seasick again almost the entire time. By the time the ship made it to Ireland to take on additional passengers, he was bedridden, and he spent the rest of the time in his cabin. He even missed his own birthday.

"I'm so sorry, Trudi," Peter murmured to his new bride. "I just don't do well on these big ships."

"It's alright. Just focus on feeling better," Trudi reassured him. "I'll find something to pass the time."

First, she decided to knit a sweater as a birthday present for Peter. Then, she wrote letters to her mother, brother, and sister. But, unfortunately, that only took a few days.

Little did she know, she would be more or less on her own for nearly two weeks.

Trudi absolutely loved to read, so she spent a good portion of the rest of her trip pouring over anything she could get her hands on. She quickly finished the two books she had brought with her, and then borrowed others from a couple of passengers she had befriended. It certainly wasn't the way she had envisioned her first trip to America with her new husband going, but it would have to do.

Every morning after she had breakfast in the dining room, she would bring Peter a cup of tea and some crackers. Then, she would make her way up to the top deck of the ship, reading material in hand, in search of a comfortable place to settle until lunch; she absolutely relished the mild weather and the fresh sea air. And every morning, one of the ship's attendants, a charming young man from Italy with straight black hair, olive skin, and gray eyes, would check on her to see if she needed anything.

"Good morning, ma'am! My name is Marco. Can I get you something?"

"No thank you, Marco," Trudi replied. I'm doing just fine."

"Well, I am here for you if you need anything." As Marco started to leave, he hesitated before turning back around.

"Ma'am, if you don't mind me asking, I've seen you here several days in a row now. Knitting and reading your books all day long. This is a wonderful ship, with so much to do. Yet here you sit. Are you traveling alone? If so, I would be happy to take some time to show you around."

Trudi blushed at the notion that the young man had taken an interest in her.

"That is very kind of you, Marco," she said. "But I am actually on my honeymoon."

"Your honeymoon?" repeated Marco, both surprised and embarrassed. "I am so sorry!"

"No, no! It's okay. My husband and I were recently married. But unfortunately, the trip is doing his stomach no favors, if you know what I mean," she politely explained. "He spends most of his time in the cabin. I feel awful for him. So I just occupy my time by reading. After all, how can I have fun knowing he's so miserable?"

"I understand, ma'am. You are such a good wife! And again, I apologize for the intrusion. Have a pleasant day. And if you need anything—anything at all—please don't hesitate to let me know."

Trudi smiled as he walked away. *Wait until I tell Frida about this!* she thought to herself.

After thirteen days at sea, the ship landed in Rotterdam, New York, and once again, Peter's cousin Werner Krause picked them up and drove them to his home in Binghamton. They visited with him and his family for a few days, and Trudi spent a lot of time getting to know his wife Renate, taking the opportunity to ask her questions about life in America, since the two of them had moved there from Germany several years earlier.

"So how do you like living here, Renate? Is it a big adjustment from back home?" Trudi asked.

"It's different," Renate replied. "I know I'm being a bit vague, but that's the best way I can describe it. Everything is different. The food. The weather. The people. The stores. Not necessarily in a bad way—I don't want to alarm you. This is a wonderful town; we really do love it here. But the truth is, I really miss home. I miss my family, of course.

My friends. I think the holidays are the most difficult time of the year."

Trudi's heart sank. She had assumed as much, but hearing it directly from someone with experience made it all too real. Perhaps a little remorse was beginning to set in.

"You'll be okay," Renate reassured her. "It may take a little time, but you will grow to love it here in the United States. I understand there is a large German population in St. Louis, so you will meet a lot of people who have been through the same thing. You can count on them for support. It's no different here. We all work together to keep our traditions alive. I belong to a women's singing group. We are also members of the German Cultural Society, which sponsors a local Oktoberfest and several concerts and dances throughout the year. I'm sure they have the same types of activities in St. Louis, so I hope you packed your dirndl!"

The thought of wearing one of her beloved dirndls, and Peter dressed in his lederhosen while dancing a polka or waltz, brought a big smile to Trudi's face.

Soon it was time to say their goodbyes, load up the car, and begin the long trek to St. Louis. Always one to plan ahead, Peter had driven his Ambassador to Binghamton prior to the wedding so they would have a reliable and convenient way to get home.

* * *

Trudi was excited about the drive to St. Louis because it would give the newlyweds an opportunity to have some of the bonding time they had missed out on while on the ship. But she soon realized the ride would not come without its challenges, as there was no easy way to get to St. Louis from Binghamton by car. The U.S. government was in the process of building its own version of the autobahn, a high-speed, interstate highway system, but the ambitious project was years away from being completed. So, they had to drive through each and every small town along the way. It took nearly five full days to complete the 1,000-mile trip halfway across the country.

By the time they reached the Mississippi River, the remorse that Trudi had begun feeling in Binghamton had returned in a major way. As she gazed out the car window during the trip, all she could focus on were the various signs of poverty and decay: streets lined with litter, patches of overgrown weeds in people's yards, paint peeling off the front of what appeared to be vacant buildings, and old, rundown vehicles parked on the side of the road. At one point, Trudi noticed a picnic table conspicuously displayed in someone's front yard, and a couple of abandoned tires and overflowing trash cans in another.

She had never seen anything like this before. Her eyes welled up with tears, but she continued staring out the window in an effort to hide her feelings from Peter. *What have I done?* she thought to herself. *If I had the money, I would turn around and go home. What a big difference this is from Ortenburg!*

"You're awful quiet over there," Peter said after a while, after sensing some tension.

"I'm just taking in the scenery," Trudi responded, continuing to stare out her window.

"Yeah, it's a little different than home."

"That is absolutely true."

Trudi's hometown of Ortenburg was quite different, indeed. Walking through the main part of town made one feel like they had just stepped into a fairytale setting. The buildings, many of which were more than 500 years old, were always in pristine condition. No one dared to leave any trash lying around. The only things littering the towns-people's properties were native plants and gorgeous flowers. The countryside surrounding the town featured rolling hills and lush valleys. Even the local cemetery resembled a botanical garden of sorts.

After another stretch of awkward silence, Peter tried to lighten the mood with some humor. "Trudi, I've got a little story for you," he began.

After Sunday service, the minister greeted his congregants at the door as they were leaving the church. Soon, young Billy, just eight years old, made his way to the front of the line.

"Reverend," said Billy. "When I get older, I'm going to give a lot of money to you and your church."

The minister replied, "That's very generous of you, Billy. But what made you think of that now?"

"Well, my father always says you're such a poor preacher!"

Peter chuckled, but Trudi turned from the window just long enough for him to see her unhappiness. Peter realized he had to find another way to make his new wife feel at ease.

"Where we are going, it's not so bad," he tried to reassure her. "Cedar Hill is a small town outside of St. Louis. But it's a fairly new area; a lot of new construction. And people seem to take care of their property, for the most part. I really think you'll like it." He paused for a moment before continuing, "But there's something you should know. The house still needs a little work."

Of course, this latest news gave Trudi no sense of relief whatsoever. She didn't dare look away from the window for fear of bursting into tears. "I'm sure it will be fine," she replied simply, trying to maintain her composure.

Soon they crossed a bridge over the mighty Mississippi River into downtown St. Louis, and Trudi could finally see a ray of hope. The city was quite busy, with workers hustling to and from lunch. Street cars and various other vehicles were stuck in traffic along narrow roads, lined on both sides with tall buildings that housed offices, shops, ware-houses, and hotels.

Peter turned down a side street, and the couple stopped for lunch at a popular diner called Crown Candy. Once inside, Trudi took special notice of the interesting décor, which featured a black-and-white checkered tile floor, smooth red tabletops, stainless steel chairs with black seat cushions, and several ornate black electric fans spinning from the ceiling above.

"Trudi, let me order for you," Peter requested. "You're going to have to try something that's uniquely American. They call it a BLT. It's unbelievable!"

"What is a BLT?" Trudi asked apprehensively.

"It stands for bacon, lettuce, and tomato. And it comes with three slices of toasted bread. Plus, they have the world's best chocolate shakes here. You have to try one!" Peter urged.

"A chocolate shake?"

"Yes. It's soft ice cream mixed with milk that they serve in a glass. You can actually drink it, but I suggest you still use a spoon."

Trudi was amazed at how acclimated to America Peter had become in such a short period of time. It gave her hope that maybe she could do the same.

"Two chocolate shakes and one BLT, please—we'll split it," Peter said to the server.

Trudi thought it rather odd that Peter would only order one sandwich for the two of them. Did he not have enough money for lunch? Had he fallen on hard times financially and hidden it from her? Her stomach began to form knots to the point that she wasn't sure she would even be able to eat anything.

"Excuse me, Peter, but I have to use the toilet."

Trudi quickly made her way across the diner and ducked inside the washroom. What she really needed was a chance to compose herself. As she looked at herself in the mirror, she was finally able to let go. The tears came streaming down her cheeks. *This is too much. Maybe I don't know Peter as well as I thought I did.* Letting out a heavy sigh, she said to herself, *Even so, you knew this wasn't going to be easy. Now pull yourself together.*

Trudi returned to the table just as the waitress was bringing out the food. It immediately became clear to her why Peter had only ordered one sandwich to share between the two of them: even divided in half, this colossal concoction was more than she could have handled on her own. In Germany, meats and cheeses were eaten accompanied by a single slice of bread. She had never had what Americans call a sandwich before. So, she was shocked to see the plate before her: loads of bacon piled on top of a huge tuft of iceberg lettuce, and several slices of tomato all mixed in between three slices of thin, toasted white bread. The sandwich, in all its glory, stood a whopping six inches tall.

Trudi looked at Peter and then at some of the other patrons in the diner to see how they attacked this massive meal. Peter, of course, immediately began to cut the sandwich down to a manageable size before using his fork to eat it one bite at a time. However, Trudi was appalled to see one customer a few tables away actually grab it with both hands and shove it into his mouth. With every bite, countless morsels fell to his plate, onto the table, and even in his lap. *Where are his manners?* Trudi thought.

Peter could see that she was shocked. "I know we don't eat that way in Germany. People here put the meat and bread together and eat it with their hands. But the sandwiches aren't usually this big," he explained. "I told you this place is different!"

They were barely able to finish their meal. Peter paid the bill, and they headed back to the car. But before reaching their final destination in Cedar Hill, the couple stopped to visit some of Peter's friends in the city, Heinz and Herta Vogel and Hermann and Greta Ruhle. They were all thrilled to finally meet Trudi and joked that Peter had married a British girl because she spoke such proper English—the King's English. This was a byproduct of Trudi having worked in London for two years.

It was becoming dark by the time the couple finally made it to Cedar Hill; as a result, Trudi couldn't get a very good feel for what her adopted hometown looked like. However, she was in for another shock when she walked through the front door of the house.

It needs "a little work"? she thought to herself. *Is he crazy? Where are the walls? It's not even close to being finished!* But, true to form, she kept her panic-fueled thoughts to herself.

Peter grabbed his hammer and drove a nail into a two-by-four so Trudi could hang up her coat. But before too long, Trudi snatched it off the nail and put it back on because the temperature was dropping significantly, and there was no furnace to keep them warm.

A few days later, it became so cold that Peter and Trudi had to stay with the Vogels for a short period of time. Although miserable on the inside, Trudi never complained.

Now Peter had to put his ingenuity to work to make the house livable. They didn't have kitchen cabinets or countertops just yet. Instead, Peter set up a few concrete blocks and laid a piece of plywood on top for a counter, and a hot plate served as a makeshift stove. Eventually, Hermann Ruhle and his boss, Mr. Richter, who were bricklayers, built a fireplace as a belated wedding present for the newlyweds so that they could finally have some heat for their home.

It was a modest, one-story frame house just 1,300 square feet in size, with a living room, a kitchen, two bedrooms, and one full bath. The exterior featured a combination of sandstone along the bottom third of the house and dark red wood veneer above. The front entrance, complete with a red six-panel door, was accented with matching stone and an oblong flower box to the right that sat below a large picture window. A concrete sidewalk would eventually connect the front door to a gravel driveway along the right side of the lot, leading downhill to a one-car garage built strategically underneath a back porch. The property backed up to a wooded common area about five acres in size, so Peter looked forward to the day he might have some free time to go deer hunting with his neighbors.

Upon entering the home, Peter's rather creative, open-air layout made it seem much larger than it really was. As one made their way through the small foyer, their eyes would immediately meet the beautiful red brick fireplace just past the entryway in the living room on the right. The fireplace actually served as the corner of the room and provided precious heat from two sides. To the right of the fireplace was an island consisting of handmade cabinetry both above and below the countertop that separated the family area from the kitchen. The bedrooms and bathroom, along with a staircase to the basement, were located on the left side of the house. A back door in the kitchen led to a screened-in porch that Peter would later convert to a third bedroom.

Trudi slowly began to make a few friends. First she met Maria and Harry, who lived two doors away, and twelve-year-old Lisa from across the street. To welcome Trudi to the neighborhood, the young girl brought her a male kitten—a mellow, loving, red tabby—that she named Schtritzi. Trudi adored animals, and always had a cat growing up. So the thoughtful gift made her feel closer to home and came into her life when she needed it the most. The ever-loyal Schtritzi quickly became Trudi's constant companion, following her throughout the house, sitting under foot as she prepared dinner, and cuddling up next to her while she was reading a book.

Soon, the cold, cruel winter began to regularly beat upon their door. The couple still needed a furnace, as the fireplace could only heat the house so much. But money was a little tight. The kitten's milk would actually freeze over from the bitter cold every night. During the day, Trudi would attempt to keep warm by racing around the house tending to the household chores, and then she and Schtritzi would huddle next to the fireplace until it was time to make dinner. But after a while, it became quite a lonely and tiresome existence for Trudi.

Fortunately, Maria came to her rescue by inviting her over for lunch every afternoon, both to have company and to stay warm. Schtritzi came too, much to the chagrin of the Becks' dachshund, Rico.

Maria grew up in the Bronx and was raised by her Jewish aunt, but she converted to Catholicism when she married Harry several years later. She never really went into much detail about her childhood with Trudi except to say that she and her mother had a falling out, and her father had been deceased for a long time. When she was twelve years old, she and her aunt moved to Missouri to live closer to relatives on her father's side of the family.

Maria wasn't just petite; she looked downright tiny—five-foot-nothing and about ninety pounds, with dark, coarse, shoulder-length hair. She was never seen without deep red lipstick adorning her face, and, whenever she and Harry went out for a special occasion, she would proudly display her collection of costume jewelry: perhaps a swathing necklace awash in aurora borealis (a type of rhinestone with an iridescent finish) or maybe a brooch with oval and pear-shaped cabochons, clip-on earrings fashioned with glass heart-shaped stones and, of course, a mix of large, ornate rings on every other finger. The East Coast influence never really left her, for she had no problem telling others exactly how it was—whether they wanted to hear it or not—in that deep, raspy, yet somehow adorable voice brought on by years of chain-smoking.

Despite Maria's rough exterior, she had a soft place in

her heart for Trudi and certainly welcomed her companionship. In addition to helping raise Harry's cousin, Wolfgang, they had a son and a daughter of their own and also looked after Harry's mentally disabled brother when his parents needed a break. Truth be told, Maria looked forward to the visits as much as Trudi did.

Maria, who loved to bake, learned that Trudi's birthday, December 8th, was coming up soon. So, after lunch that day, she eagerly surprised Trudi with a homemade birthday cake to celebrate the big day. Trudi was extremely touched by her new friend's thoughtful gesture, for she had been feeling rather homesick. After all, this was her first birthday since moving away from her family. Christmas was just around the corner, too.

Much like Maria, Harry was a short, slender man who worked as a letter carrier in their neighborhood. He was born in Germany but came to the United States with his parents as an infant. Unfortunately, neither he nor Maria could hold a conversation with the Mayers in their native German. A man of few words, Harry could always be found with a cigar hanging out of his mouth, though he wasn't always actually smoking it. And although he could be rather gruff to those around him, he most certainly had a good heart.

CHAPTER 12

By the end of the year, Peter and Trudi learned that they were going to be parents. So, Peter felt a new sense of urgency to complete construction of the house. There was no time for leisure. Instead, evenings and weekends were spent working on the house, and Trudi—and Schtritzi, of course—were right there alongside Peter. One day, when Trudi was helping Peter install the siding on the exterior of the house, the kitten climbed the ladder and sat down beside the pregnant Trudi, as if to make sure she was okay.

As her due date approached, Trudi continued to help Peter as he feverishly put the finishing touches on their home. Along came the month of July and their first Independence Day together in the United States. Trudi stood on a ladder helping Peter hang drywall, doing the best she could to hold it in place while he fastened it to the studs with a hammer and nails.

"Trudi, hold it steady," Peter said. "Just a couple more nails and we'll be done with this one. Trudi, c'mon. Hold it right!"

"I think my water broke," Trudi stated calmly. "The baby is coming. We need to go to the hospital. Right now."

"Oh, my!" Peter exclaimed. "Okay. Okay. I'm sorry. One more nail—there! Okay, that should do it. Let's get you down from there."

Peter carefully helped his wife down the ladder and grabbed her suitcase from the bedroom. Then the two of them left for the hospital.

Appropriately, their first child, a boy, was born on the Fourth of July, 1957. He did not arrive without complications, however. Peter had misunderstood how much he would owe for the delivery and the subsequent hospital stay. He didn't have enough money in the bank, and the doctor would not release Trudi and the baby without being paid in full. Peter didn't dare contact his father for money. Instead, he called upon his cousin Josef to help him out. Josef immediately wired the funds from Indianapolis so that Peter could take his new family home.

"I'll pay you back as soon as I can," Peter reassured him.

"It is not a problem," Josef responded. "You have more important things to worry about right now, so take your time."

After a short pause, Josef continued, "By the way, I have some news of my own. I am engaged to be married!"

"Are you kidding me, Josef? I didn't even know you were seriously dating anyone," Peter responded, shocked.

"Well, I will admit that it happened very quickly," said Josef. "The last time I was visiting Memmingen on vacation, I saw a green Volkswagen Beetle driving through the streets. I had no idea who the driver was, but I was curious because green is a very unusual color for a Volkswagen. A few months later, after I returned to Indianapolis, I spied the same green Volkswagen near my neighborhood. Can you believe it? So, I was more determined than ever to learn who owned that car. One day, I followed it to the grocery store and introduced myself to the owner. Much to my surprise, it was owned by a lovely woman named Lena Koenig. She is from Indianapolis, but her parents live in Germany. I asked Lena to dinner, and the rest is history! I'm also taking your advice and building a new house of my own. I've been looking for property for some time now, and I finally found a piece of land for sale in an undeveloped area near a farmer's field. The property is absolutely beautiful. It sits on a hillside and overlooks a magnificent creek. It reminds me of Germany, so I know Lena and I will love living there."

"That's wonderful news, Josef! I'm very happy for you. So, tell me about this girl," Peter urged.

"Well, she's several years older than me," said Josef. "She has two children from a previous marriage—a son and a daughter, who are both in their early twenties. I know we're not going to be able to have children together, but that's alright. I love her, and so it doesn't matter. I suspect my parents were hoping I would have a family of my own, but it's just not meant to be. It's okay."

"You know that Trudi and I wish you all the best," said Peter. "I can't wait to meet Lena. In the meantime, thank you again for agreeing to help me out with Trudi and the baby."

"I'm just happy I could do it. What is the baby's name?" Josef asked.

Peter paused before solemnly replying, "Martin—after my brother."

"Perfect," said Josef. "Your father will be extremely proud."

Unfortunately, the tough times didn't end there for Peter and Trudi. By the early sixties, the couple had had three children—Martin, Sophie, and Karin—and they were still finding that money was hard to come by. When Peter left for work every morning, the only money he carried with him was a dime he kept in his lunch pail just in case he needed to make an emergency phone call.

A downturn in the local construction industry eventually led to Peter being laid off from his job at Guild Craftsman. He turned to the Union Hall for work, but jobs were difficult to find there, too. He and his family had no source of income, but the bills still needed to be paid every month.

So, once again, a desperate Peter called upon his cousin Josef—not his father—to borrow some cash just to make the house payment. Even though Peter's father was wealthy, asking him for money was never an option. Peter wouldn't do that. He was a humble man, and he was absolutely determined to make it on his own. If he had requested help from his father, it would, to him, have been an admission of failure, and his father would have insisted that he come home for good. The truth is, if they did go back home, he and Trudi would have been much better off financially—with a big house, a successful job, and all the privileges that came with being a Mayer living in Memmingen. Peter's father certainly had the influence to make it all happen.

Fortunately, it never got to that point. The economy eventually improved, and Peter's employment prospects soared as a result. The union gave him opportunities to work as a finish carpenter in some of the fanciest office buildings and most popular restaurants in St. Louis. Thus, his handiwork graced extravagant boardrooms and elegant bars alike.

Still, he and Trudi remained frugal when it came to money. For instance, Trudi made most of the children's clothing herself. And, with the exception of Christmas-time, they rarely called home, choosing instead to communicate with family by mail because it was quite expensive to place phone calls overseas.

As Renate Krause had predicted on Trudi's first day in America, Christmas proved to be a very difficult time of year for the Mayers—especially Trudi. Every time she heard the hymn "Silent Night" during the holidays, it would remind her of home, and the tears would flow.

Although Trudi and Peter deeply missed their families and traditions, their siblings and parents did their very best to bring Germany to them. Their children especially looked forward to receiving wonderful care packages from their relatives during the holiday season each year. Peter's and Trudi's respective families would send treats, homemade clothes for the kids, delightful keepsakes, and well wishes. The Mayers would also receive gifts through the mail from their relatives in Binghamton and Indianapolis.

To compensate for some of the emptiness she felt, Trudi worked hard to maintain certain family traditions. For instance, she used her mother's recipes to bake home-made Christmas cookies for friends and family. The fine delicacies included round jelly-topped creations sprinkled with ground pecans and powdered sugar; snowball-like concoctions mixed with mini chocolate chips; thin, square, chocolate shortbreads capped with white icing; and small, circular sandwich cookies—complete with raspberry preserves squished between two slices of cookie crust.

Peter, ever the meticulous craftsman, fashioned an exceptionally realistic manger scene that he displayed under the Christmas tree every year. He transformed some old pieces of scrap wood he found in his basement workshop to create the structure, which was complete with a short fence on both sides and two troughs filled with seeds to emulate animal feed. He retrieved several small rocks from the backyard along with a bit of foliage trimmed from a nearby arborvitae shrub and positioned them around the structure, as well. Then, he sprinkled some pieces of straw throughout the base of the display. Only the wooden figurines themselves had come from a store.

Despite the distance from family, Peter also tried to recreate his childhood Christmas Eve experience for his children. His fondest memory came as a five-year-old. The drawing room back home, complete with a Christmas tree and gifts, remained off-limits for the entire day. The wait seemed excruciatingly long for a small child. Then, promptly at 6:00 p.m., his father would ceremoniously open the doors to a magical scene—a ten-foot-high balsam illuminated by the flames of two dozen or so red candles and adorned with precious ornaments made of pewter, glass, and hand-painted figurines, towering over a sea of beautifully wrapped packages carefully positioned underneath.

One ornament, in particular, always seemed to mesmerize Peter as a child. It was a small, three-dimensional star of Bethlehem that his birth mother, Erna, had handmade from narrow strips of white paper. Peter was fascinated by its intricate design—several points of varying lengths protruding in different directions, all created from precise folds and miraculously held together without the need for tape or glue. Many years later, his own tree in Cedar Hill would be adorned with similar gems, as Trudi had learned how to make these special types of ornaments from her own mother as well.

One Christmas in his childhood, Peter scanned the gifts quickly as he dashed through the doorway. Eventually, he saw it—the largest package in the room—and it had his name on it. "Could it be?" he wondered. As his imagination ran wild and he began to reach for the package, he was interrupted by a stern voice. "No gifts yet!" his father reminded him. "First we sing; then, we open gifts."

Peter quickly found a seat on the floor a few feet away, but he could hardly contain himself, anxiously sitting through the family Christmas concert while barely mouthing the words to each hymn. Finally, the last note was sung, and everyone's attention turned to Peter's father, who always handed out the gifts one at a time to each member of the family.

"Gerhard, let's start with you," Heinrich said to his eldest son. Peter, disappointed that he wasn't chosen first, watched his brother open a long, narrow package with extreme curiosity. *Wow, an air rifle!* Peter thought to himself. Little did he know at the time, but that same rifle would come back to haunt him a few years later.

Young Erna was next. Much to her delight, she received a doll and a baby carriage. Peter began to squirm with excitement as he waited for his turn. Mercifully, his father finally pointed to the large box under the tree. "Peter, that one's for you," he declared.

As Peter jumped to his feet and hurried toward the tree, the box seemed to grow bigger and bigger. Soon, he pounced on the package, ripped off the wrapping paper into countless pieces, and became overcome with excitement upon what was revealed: a toy car featuring a steering wheel, pedals, and a seat—one that he could actually drive on the sidewalk!

"What a great gift, Peter!" his brother Martin acknowledged. "You are going to be the most popular boy on Sommerstrasse."

Because of dear memories such as this one, Peter always made sure his own children had a similar experience on Christmas Eve—even during tough times.

The family spent Christmas of 1960 in Germany when Peter's youngest brother Reinhold got married. The wedding took place right after Christmas, so Heinrich paid for the entire clan to travel to Germany for the event.

Although they didn't have any family members living nearby, Peter and Trudi made some very close friends in St. Louis, including the Vogels and the Ruhles. So, they would host various neighbors and friends at their home not only during the holidays but also throughout the rest of the year.

Another one of Renate Krause's predictions came true, as Peter and Trudi discovered a dozen or so German social clubs in town. These groups afforded German immigrants the opportunity to indulge in traditions from back home. Peter and Trudi heard from some of their friends about organizations such as the Schwaben Singing Society and the Liederkranz Singing Society. Additionally, Peter reconnected with the German Cultural Society. Every few months, they held a dance or another social event where one could meet new people. But it wasn't until the kids got a little older that Peter and Trudi officially joined any of these groups. Peter happened to work with several people who were very active in some of these fellowship organizations, and they finally talked him into getting involved. Soon he became active too, and a valuable member, at that. Because when a group owns a facility and a member happens to be a carpenter, their services are often needed to help with the upkeep and repairs.

Peter also made sure to keep in touch with his old friend Georg as much as possible, especially during the holidays. Although Georg had moved to California several years earlier, the two remained close for a while. Suddenly, however, contact from Georg mysteriously came to a halt. Peter tried calling his friend two or three times over Christmas, but he received no response. He began to worry. *Something's not right,* he thought. *Georg is pretty good about staying in touch. God, I hope everything's okay.*

He tried calling again after the holidays, thinking maybe Georg had traveled home to Germany to be with family, but there was still no answer.

"Maybe you should write to his family," suggested Trudi. Although she had never met Georg, she knew what the friendship meant to Peter, and she began to worry alongside him.

Peter agreed, and promptly composed a letter to Georg's sister, Helga, who lived in Ulm, Germany. Then he waited for a reply. And waited. And waited.

It took several weeks, but he finally received a response from Helga.

Dear Peter:

Thank you for your letter. It was a pleasure to hear from

you after all these years!

It is with great sorrow that I must tell you that my dear brother Georg has passed away.

Peter's heart sank and his eyes welled with tears as he struggled to read on.

He died from cancer three days before Christmas. It went rather quickly. He was diagnosed back in October. The news, obviously, came as a complete surprise. He hadn't been feeling well for many weeks. By the time he went to a doctor, they said there wasn't anything they could do for him. As a result, he became quite depressed and reclusive. It didn't take long after that.

No one knows for sure what happened, but I really think it had something to do with his job. As you know, he went to California to become a professional photographer, but that didn't work out. So he took a job with a company that tested rockets. He would spend his days using x-ray equipment to make sure the welded joints were safe and secure. I always worried about that. How safe could it be? Unfortunately, there's nothing that can be done about it now.

We are all heartbroken, as no one from our family was able to see him before he died.

I know the two of you were close, having ventured to America together. Of course, none of us wanted Georg to leave home at that time, but we were comforted in knowing he was not going alone. Please know that he cherished your friendship.

I wish you and your family all the best, and I hope we can visit the next time you travel to Germany.

Regards,
Helga

CHAPTER 13

One day at work, as Peter was tacking a strip of baseboard to the wall, he heard a harrowing noise off in the distance. He was well aware of the types of sirens used by police cars, ambulances, and fire trucks, but this was like nothing he had ever heard before.

"What's that?" he asked no one in particular.

"Those are tornado sirens," his boss replied.

Suddenly, Peter had a flashback to the air raid sirens he had experienced as a child back home during the war. Instinctively, his muscles tightened, and he clenched his jaw.

"What do we do?" he wondered. "Is there some type of shelter we go to?"

"No. It's just some wind and rain. Nothing to worry about," his boss replied dismissively. "Keep working. We've got a deadline to meet."

Peter returned to his task as his boss left the room, but he couldn't shake the feeling of dread he felt in the pit of his stomach.

About twenty minutes later, Peter felt the room begin

to rumble and shake. He knew something wasn't right and instinctively sprang to his feet. "I'm getting out of here!" he declared. The three other members of his crew nodded in agreement and followed closely behind as he ran into the hallway and then to a stairwell a few feet away. Seconds later, the roof caved in right where they had been working. Wisely, the men hunkered down in the stairwell and waited out the rest of the storm, thinking it would be better to stay put than to venture outside. Several minutes later, welcome silence enveloped them, and they decided that it was finally safe to leave the premises. They picked their way around the damage: a mangled ladder, shards of broken glass, and some sawhorses, lumber, and scraps of drywall strewn across the floor. They called out to any potentially fallen co-workers. Hearing none, the grateful men escaped to the street, where debris littered the area as far as the eye could see.

The tornado had followed a morning of torrential rains, flash-flooding, hail, and winds up to sixty-five miles per hour, and had literally changed the landscape before Peter's eyes. When he arrived at the job site first thing that morning, everything around him had appeared normal—drenched, but normal. Now, just a few hours later, the area was almost unrecognizable to him. Mass destruction ruled the land—once again reminding him of the tremendous damage that had been inflicted on Memmingen during the war. Only this time, Mother Nature was the enemy. Lucky to be alive, numerous people wandered around in a daze. No one knew quite what to do or where to go.

Before Peter could process all of this, he was startled by the frantic screams of a woman in her thirties, Mildred

Thomas, who lived with her six children across the street.

"Help! Somebody! Please help me!" the battered woman pleaded, waving one arm for attention as she held on tightly to her seven-month-old son in the other. Her eyes locked on Peter's. She quickly reached for the hand of another young child, her two-year-old daughter, and ran toward him from her front yard.

"My kids! Oh my God, I can't find the rest of my kids! Please help!"

Peter nodded, lightly touching her arm in reassurance before racing toward the pile of rubble that had once served as the southwest corner of the Thomas home. He quickly scanned the mess but couldn't see any obvious signs of life—only a battered structure and countless bricks and wooden boards strewn about. Half the roof was missing. Every windowpane had been shattered, and a towering oak tree from the front yard had snapped in two, leaving nothing but a three-foot-high stump protruding out of the ground. Part of the home had caved in, and four of Mildred's six children were caught somewhere in the ruins. Immediately, Peter's three co-workers joined him in the search—and hopefully, the rescue—of the children.

"Is anyone there?" Peter shouted into the rubble. "Can you hear us?"

Once again, Mildred started to scream, so Peter turned his head toward her and put a finger to his lips in an effort to calm her down so he could try to hear a response.

"Kids, are you there?" he asked again.

Suddenly, a faint response emanated from the wreckage about twenty feet from where Peter and the other men stood.

"Robby? Is that you?" Mildred cried in reply. "David?

Sissy? Tina? Are you there?"

"Over there!" shouted Tom, one of Peter's colleagues, as he pointed toward the corner of the house. "I think that's the kitchen. Someone's under the table."

As the four men cautiously picked their way through the maze of damage, the children's cries became louder. Soon, they reached the table, which had been miraculously shielded on one side by the toppled refrigerator. After dragging the hefty appliance away, the men began to carefully remove the other debris on and around it. Suddenly, a small head poked out from underneath. Then a second, a third, and finally, a fourth. All the children had bumps, scrapes, and cuts, but Sissy, who was lying on the ground, seemed to be the most injured. She appeared to have a broken leg, so Peter reached down, gently scooped her up into his arms, and carried her back to her mother, who was waiting anxiously in the street.

While the men didn't say anything among themselves, they were all thinking the same thing. That bulky fridge could have easily slammed on top of the table, killing them all. Instead, somehow, it had happened to land just right— and may have actually saved their lives.

At that moment, a couple of firefighters reached the group and began administering first aid to the children. Fortunately, none of their injuries were life-threatening.

Just a few blocks away, however, other victims of the tornado's destructive path hadn't been so lucky. Another house, located at the corner of Delmar Boulevard and Whittier Street, had been completely destroyed by the storm. Eight people died in the collapse.

Once the excitement of the rescue subsided and Peter was able to catch his breath, all he could think about was

Trudi and the kids. *Did the storm hit Cedar Hill?* he wondered. *Are they safe? They must be worried and afraid, and I'm not there to protect them.*

That evening, it would take Peter almost three hours to finally reach home. Unable to call because the phone lines were out of service, the trip seemingly lasted a lifetime. Along the way, he saw similar destruction. But the farther away he drove from the city, the better everything looked. By the time he made it to the Cedar Hill city limits, everything seemed normal again. "No tornado here! I can't believe it. Thank you, Oh Lord!" he exclaimed.

As he pulled into the driveway, Trudi and the kids came running out the front door to greet him with hugs and kisses.

"We were so worried. Thank God you're home!" Trudi cried.

"You have no idea," Peter replied. Thank God, indeed.

The brutal tornado had roared through the heart of St. Louis and was the third-deadliest in the city's history, having toppled a local television tower and tossed it onto a neighboring apartment building before tearing off a large section of the roof from a nearby sports arena. The worst storm experienced by area residents in thirty-two years, it killed twenty-one people and injured 345, in addition to damaging more than 1,700 homes and businesses.

* * *

With another child on the way in 1963, a girl named Elisabeth, Peter began construction of a new, larger house on the lot next door. Since the day he had purchased both lots years earlier, his plan had been to build a starter home on the smaller, odd-shaped lot and a second house on the nicer one.

It took about a year to complete the new house, and the family moved in just in time to welcome Peter's father and Reinhold for a visit. The guests saw firsthand the type of life that the couple had built for themselves, and came to accept that their ever-deepening roots and long-term goals would most likely keep them tethered to America.

But that didn't stop Heinrich from trying one last time to lure his son and family back home several months later. The sport of bowling had become extremely popular in Germany, and Peter's father had learned of an opportunity to purchase a bowling establishment on the outskirts of Memmingen. He urged his son to come for a visit to check it out. So, Peter made a brief trip to Germany to appease his father.

"Peter, this is the perfect business for you," his father told him. "I can help you with the purchase, and you can manage the operation. It has the potential to be extremely profitable. There's nothing else like it in Memmingen."

While Peter had reluctantly considered other opportunities presented to him by his father in the past, this one far and away appealed to him the most.

"It sounds pretty good, Father. I'll talk to Trudi about it when I get back to Cedar Hill, and then you and I can work out the details. Who knows? Maybe it's time to come home."

But shortly after Peter returned home from Germany, tragedy struck.

It started out as a typical Saturday morning. Trudi had taken the car for her weekly visit to the grocery store. With their mother away from the house, the children were expected to use their time wisely and clean up their bedrooms. Peter was down in the basement, sharpening his garden tools in anticipation of a long day of yard work. Suddenly, his solitude was broken by Martin and Sophie racing down the basement steps in a ruckus.

"Dad! DAD!" they yelled in unison. "There's a police officer at the front door!"

"The police? What the hell..." Peter stopped mid-sentence and hustled up the staircase, leaping up the steps two at a time. The children hurried behind him in an attempt to keep up. When he came around the corner, he saw a tall, imposing figure standing inside the front door. The man wore a tan dress shirt adorned with a shiny silver badge, dark brown slacks, freshly polished black boots, and, of course, a large black belt sporting a handgun in its holster. As Peter slowly approached the officer, he hoped that the issue he was there for was a simple misunderstanding.

"Mr. Mayer?" the officer greeted him. "Good morning. I'm Officer Hickel of the Jefferson County Sheriff's Department. Can I talk to you outside?"

Peter knew then that this was no mistake.

"Kids, stay here. I'll be right back," Peter gently ordered them as he closed the door behind him.

"Is something wrong, officer?" Peter asked apprehensively upon closing the door to his house.

"I'm afraid I have some bad news," the officer replied. "Your wife is Trudi, correct?"

Peter nodded.

"Your wife's been in an automobile accident."

"No. No, that can't be right. She just ran to the store. Are you sure?"

"Unfortunately yes, sir. It just happened about twenty minutes ago. It was a bad accident. A delivery truck ran a red light at Old Post Road and T-boned her car. She's hurt pretty bad. The paramedics treated her on the scene and are now taking her to the ER at St. Anthony's."

Peter's face had turned ashen with fear as he listened, and his heart sank into the pit of his stomach.

"Sir, you need to be with her. Why don't you get your things, and I'll take you to the hospital."

Peter stood there for a few seconds, staring out at the front yard in shock and disbelief. Numerous thoughts raced through his mind as he faced the possibility of having to endure another agonizing loss: *How bad is it? Surely she'll be okay, right? What about the kids? I can't lose Trudi after all this. I can't do it. She has to be okay. We're supposed to have a life here. Together. With our family. Oh my God, what...*

"Sir. Uh, Mr. Mayer?" the officer interrupted. "Sir, we have to get going. Now."

Peter snapped out of his daze and shouted for the kids as he flung open the front screen door. Once inside, his eyes met those of his confused and frightened children.

"Dad, what's the matter?" asked Sophie.

"Mom had an accident with the car, but she's okay." Peter tried to reassure them—and himself—that this was true. "Put on your shoes. I'm going to take you all up to Maria's house. You'll stay there while I go to your mother. Hurry! We need to go."

After the children were dropped off at the Becks' house, Officer Hickel rushed Peter to the hospital. Although the officer used his emergency lights and sirens to their advantage, the trip seemed never-ending. Peter said nothing the entire way. All he could do was look straight ahead and think about Trudi, his lifelong friend and cherished spouse. Initially, he tried to visualize the accident, but that was much too painful. So instead, he reflected on some of the memorable times they had spent together: picking berries as kids in Memmingen; the day he asked her to marry him; the stressful drive from Binghamton to Cedar Hill; the look on her face when she walked into the unfinished house; and the pure joy in her eyes when she first held their firstborn child, Martin, after giving birth in the hospital.

Now here she was again in that same hospital. Only this time, instead of bringing life, she was fighting for her own.

As the trip to the hospital continued, Peter also couldn't help but reflect on another memory of Trudi. Trudi was known to have premonitions about certain things. She had a knack for knowing that something—usually something bad—had happened before anyone even mentioned it to her. One time, she told Peter about a dream she had had the night before. She was with their neighbor, Joe Pranger. He was asking her for help because he was freezing to death. It was all she could do to cover him in blanket upon blanket in an attempt to warm him up. Minutes after telling Peter about this dream, the phone rang. It was Joe's wife, Marta, calling to tell them that Joe had been hospitalized with an infection. His fever was so high that the doctors had laid him on a bed of ice in an attempt to bring his temperature back down.

Another time, while Trudi was preparing breakfast, she noticed that one of her plants in the kitchen was wilting terribly. She knew instantly that something was wrong. A few hours later, she received a phone call from Germany that one of her sick relatives had died. In reply, she said, "I've been waiting for your call."

Peter finally reached the hospital, but the answers to his many questions came slowly. He waited for several hours in the ER before he received any news from the doctors. There he sat, alone. There was no one to reassure him that everything would be alright. It was a dark, lonely time for the young husband and father. And, for the first time, he had an inkling of what his own father had gone through years before on the day of Peter's birth. Waiting. Hoping. Praying that the person he loved most would pull through.

"Mr. Mayer?" A deep, gentle voice interrupted his pensive state, and Peter sprang to his feet. "Hello, Mr. Mayer. I'm Dr. Reynolds. Please come with me."

The doctor ushered Peter into a small office located just off the main lobby of the ER waiting room. As the doctor flipped on the light switch and closed the door behind him, Peter braced himself for the most important news of his life—his fists clenched, his jaw tight, his brow furrowed, and his body paralyzed in fear.

"Mr. Mayer, the truth is, your wife is lucky to be alive. She is stable for now, but she's still in pretty bad shape. She has a broken pelvis, a broken arm, a collapsed lung, and a fractured skull that is causing some bleeding on the brain, so that's a major concern. Until we can get that under control, I'm afraid she's not out of the woods."

A stunned Peter struggled to process what he had just heard.

"I'm terribly sorry. We're doing everything we can to help her. I'll let you know when we have an update on her condition."

"Wait, doctor," Peter blurted. "Can I see her?"

"We're moving her up to the ICU. Once they get her settled in, someone will come down and escort you to her room. Until then, please wait here."

Peter returned to the waiting room and slumped back into his seat. Although his beloved Trudi was alive, the future was no clearer than before.

About an hour later, he was finally able to see his wife. While he had braced himself for a terrible sight, her condition was still a shock to him as he stood in the doorway. She was barely conscious. The left side of her face was bruised and battered by the impact of the truck. Multiple cuts from shards of windshield glass littered her lovely face, and an oxygen mask had been placed over her mouth and nose, so she couldn't speak. A splint immobilized her left arm, and a light blue surgical cap covered her head. Tubes. Wires. IVs. It seemed as if any and every type of medical gadget available was somehow connected to poor Trudi.

Peter held back tears as he slowly approached his wife's bedside. But before he could reach her, the gentle hand of a nurse touched his elbow. "Mr. Mayer?" she said. "I'm afraid you can't stay but a few minutes. She really needs her rest. And we have more tests to do."

Peter nodded, then reached for Trudi's right hand. It felt cold and weak, but she managed to squeeze his hand ever so slightly. "It's gonna be okay. I'm here," Peter told her.

There he stood, bent over the bed rail, until the nurse told him that it was time to leave. He gently kissed her on the forehead and slowly made his way out of the room.

After some trying times over a period of several days that Peter spent wondering whether Trudi would live or die, she made enough progress to be moved to a standard hospital room. Eventually, she was transferred to a rehabilitation facility adjacent to the hospital. Then, finally, she was back home for good.

It would take nearly three months for Trudi to fully recover from her injuries. In the meantime, the bowling business opportunity in Germany that Heinrich had championed disappeared. The owner couldn't wait for Peter's decision. Another person had made an offer that was too good to pass up.

Maybe the Mayers were destined to stay in America after all.

CHAPTER 14

Peter looked at the alarm clock on his nightstand in disbelief. It said 3:14—in the a.m. He could hear a symphony of crickets performing through the open window, seemingly taunting him throughout his sleepless ordeal. He rolled back over and gazed at Trudi lying next to him. "Mom," he whispered. They had called each other Mom and Dad ever since Martin was born. "Mom, are you asleep?" But there was no response. He exhaled in frustration, wondering how she could possibly sleep under these circumstances.

Peter rolled back over and eased out of bed, careful not to wake Trudi. He shuffled out of the bedroom and slowly made his way down the hall to the bathroom for the third time in as many hours. Once inside, he flipped on the light switch and fumbled for a glass as his eyes adjusted to the brightly lit room. While filling the glass at the sink, he leaned forward and stared intently at himself in the mirror. He saw a tall, lean, physically fit, thirty-six-year-old man with a thin face, a strong chin, blue eyes, sandy brown hair, and a ruddy complexion looking back at him.

His hairline was already starting to recede. Before long, he would be just as bald as his father.

"Do I really want to do this?" Peter asked himself for the umpteenth time as he continued to look at his reflection. He knew the answer, yet he couldn't help but think about his father—specifically, how devastated he would be upon hearing the news.

Peter took a sip of water and headed back to bed. "Lousy crickets," he mumbled as his head hit the pillow. Trudi uttered a soft, yet unintelligible response. "Mom?" Peter asked again.

Trudi rolled to her side, facing him, and returned to her dreams.

As Peter watched his wife sleep, a sense of peace came over him. She was a devoted wife and mother—a modest, selfless, dignified woman who always put her family first and made those around her feel at home. Because of her, he would never be alone. They were in this together—they always had been, and there was no way that was going to change now.

At this realization, a gentle smile came across Peter's face, and he was able to finally close his eyes and relax. Before he knew it, those "lousy crickets" weren't bothering him anymore, and he soon drifted off to sleep.

* * *

Peter awoke to the rich aroma of freshly brewed coffee, letting out a big yawn and turning to the clock. Startled by what he saw, he threw off the covers and sprung out of bed. After fumbling for his slippers and pulling them on, he rushed to the kitchen and exclaimed to his wife, "It's 7:20, Mom! Why didn't you wake me up?"

"You were sound asleep. I didn't want to disturb you," replied Trudi.

"But we have to get ready. We don't want to be late!"

"We don't have to be there until noon, Dad," Trudi replied as she shook her head. "We have plenty of time. Relax and have a seat."

She took the coffee pot from the stove and brought it to the kitchen table, filled two cups nearly to the brim, then placed the pot on a potholder. The table was set with the usual morning fare: soft-boiled eggs, butter, honey, semmeln, and, of course, "Oma Cake"—a cinnamon-flavored bread baked with almonds and raisins on the inside and drizzled with a touch of white icing on top. Trudi's mother had taught her how to make the tasty treat when she was a young girl.

Trudi left the room to wake the kids. "Time to get up, everyone. Breakfast is ready!" Peter heard her declare from down the hall.

We're still going to be late, Peter thought. His father had always said you were late for an appointment even if you were fifteen minutes early. There was so much to do. They had to eat, clean up from breakfast, shower, get dressed, load the kids into the car, and drive forty-five minutes to downtown. And God forbid they encountered any traffic. Better to leave at least an hour and a half early. Noon would be here before they knew it, and Peter wasn't about to take that lightly.

He added a touch of cream to his coffee, took a careful sip so as not to burn his tongue, and turned his attention back to the spread on the table. Trudi always had a way of making every meal seem special. Everything had to be just right, from the crystal serving dishes, to the silverware and the white linen napkins, to the bouquet of freshly cut daisies prominently displayed at the center of the table. These things always reminded him of his life back home.

* * *

Heidi, the Mayers' new pet beagle, leaped from her perch on the couch and raced over to the front window in the living room, excitedly barking, quaking, wagging her tail, and leaving nose prints all over the glass.

"They're here!" an antsy Peter yelled down the hall to Trudi and the children as he hurried to the front door and opened it well before the doorbell could be rung.

"Good morning, Peter!" greeted Maria.

"Morning, Pete," said Harry.

"Hello. C'mon in," Peter replied. "Thanks again for doing this. Trudi and I really appreciate it."

"No problem! Are you ready for the big day?" Harry asked him.

"I think so." Peter checked his watch and glanced up at the wall clock just to be sure that the time was accurate. "If we don't hurry, we're going to be late. Mom! Kids! Harry and Maria are here. It's time to go!"

Peter left the Becks in the living room with Heidi and strode down the hallway to the master bedroom. He stopped for a minute to check his necktie in the mirror over Trudi's dresser before grabbing his dark suit coat from the closet. Trudi, who had been in the girls' room, entered just in time to help him slip his left arm into the sleeve.

"Relax, Dad. It's going to be fine—WE are going to be

fine," Trudi assured him as she patted him on the shoulder.

"Are the kids ready? Let's go," Peter replied.

As if on cue, all four children marched out of their bedrooms behind their parents, down the hallway, and eagerly greeted the Becks with hugs near the front door. Martin was now nine years old, Sophie was eight, Karin was six, and the baby of the family, Elisabeth, was only three.

Heidi, in response to all the excitement, bolted for the front door in hopes of not being left behind.

"Sorry, Heidi!" said Sophie, stopping her as they all headed out the door. "You can't go with us today. But we'll be home as soon as we can."

Peter strode ahead, pulling the family station wagon out of the garage behind the house and bringing it up the driveway before stopping at the curb to let the family pile in. He didn't dare risk anyone getting carsick while riding in the back of the station wagon, so he had asked the Becks to follow him in their car as they made their way downtown.

Peter had entertained the idea of becoming an American citizen ever since he finished boot camp back in 1954, knowing that doing so wouldn't necessarily mean that he would never move back to Germany. But after he got married, he decided to wait for Trudi, who had to live for a minimum of five years in the States and remain in good standing in order to become a citizen. Peter could have been given citizenship a lot sooner because he had been living here for a few years already. In his mind, though, there was never any hurry, because the only difference between citizenship and non-citizenship was the right to vote.

"I don't know who to vote for anyway!" he would always joke.

Peter and Trudi had not taken any classes to help them prepare for the test, so they studied an American civics book together instead. They had to be familiar with U.S. history, government, and other facts that were second nature to most Americans. Thanks to hours of preparation, both of them felt rather confident upon completing their tests. Still, they weren't about to take anything for granted.

Weeks later, two official letters from the U.S. government arrived in the mail. Peter knew exactly what the letters were about. And this time, unlike years earlier when he and Georg had received their draft notices, he could read them for himself. They carried the exciting and relieving news that he and Trudi had both passed their citizenship tests.

And the day of their naturalization ceremony, May 5, 1966, was finally here.

As the family drove downtown to the ceremony, Trudi, as usual, remained fairly quiet except to point out various landmarks to the kids along the way. This gave Peter a lot of time to think about the journey that had led him to this point. He was both excited and a bit apprehensive, for he hadn't breathed a word of his and Trudi's plans to his father. But that was an issue for another day. Instead, he spent some time reminiscing about his original voyage to New York, his first day on the job in St. Louis, getting drafted into the army and enduring eight weeks of boot camp, marrying Trudi and bringing her to America for the first time, the birth of his children, and the death of his dear friend Georg.

Suddenly, a tiny voice from the back seat interrupted

his trip down memory lane. "I'm bored! Are we almost there?" an impatient Elisabeth complained.

"Almost, babe," Trudi reassured her. "Just a few more minutes. Look, there is the Old Courthouse. It's over one hundred years old and features the first wrought- and cast-iron dome ever built. Isn't it beautiful? The dome was modeled after St. Peter's Basilica in Rome. And it's where the Dred Scott case took place back in the mid-1800s."

"Dred Scott? Who's that?" asked Sophie.

"Dred Scott and his wife Harriet were slaves who sued for their freedom," explained Trudi. "The judge ruled in their favor and granted them freedom. However, the case was appealed all the way to the United States Supreme Court. The court decided that slaves were property, and therefore, they had no right to sue. As a result, they had to go back into slavery for many more years. The decision accelerated the start of the Civil War. Dred and Harriet Scott wanted freedom and the ability to become U.S. citizens—just like us. Unfortunately, it didn't come so easy for them."

"You sure know a lot about American history," Peter said to his wife. "No wonder you did so well on the citizenship test! Must be all that reading you do."

Trudi nodded and smiled.

"Is that where we're going—the Old Courthouse?" asked Karin.

"No, I believe it's a museum now. We're going just up the street to a newer courthouse," Trudi explained. "It's right up here around the corner."

Peter pulled into a parking garage adjacent to the building. The Becks found a spot there as well, and everyone went inside together.

The ceremony took place in an actual courtroom at the United States Courthouse. Several other petitioners, each of whom had a sponsor, participated in the ceremony as well. Maria served as Trudi's sponsor, and Harry served as Peter's. Peter and Trudi joined the other petitioners in the jury section of the courtroom, while the sponsors and family members sat in the gallery.

Soon, everyone stood as the judge entered the room.

"Welcome, petitioners, sponsors, and guests. This is a special day, and I am honored to preside over these proceedings. Please continue standing for the singing of *God Bless America.*"

With that, a young lady sang beautifully for the group. Then, everyone sat down, and the ceremony began.

As the guest speaker, an assistant U.S. attorney, began his remarks, Trudi took Peter's hand and smiled at him. Peter gave her a nod and squeezed her hand in return.

"Today, you become an equal to all United States citizens, even those who have a long history here and those who were born here," the speaker began. "Our country is strengthened by our immigrant history. It is what makes this nation so great. Just as our forefathers came here, so have you. Others, too, have paved the way and done great things—people like Albert Einstein, Irving Berlin, and Andrew Carnegie, just to name a few."

Peter's mind began to wander as he once again thought of his family back in Germany and the path that had led him to this moment. Before his attention strayed further, however, he caught himself and refocused on the speaker.

"To put it all in perspective, I'd like to share a quote with you from George Washington, the father of our great country:

"The bosom of America is open to receive not only the Opulent and respected Stranger, but the oppressed and persecuted of all Nations and Religions; whom we shall welcome to a participation of all our rights and privileges..."

He continued, "As citizens, you have numerous rights and responsibilities. Especially the right to vote—may your voices be heard!"

Peter chuckled silently at this.

"Representatives from the League of Women Voters are located in the hallway outside this room. I encourage you to take full advantage of this opportunity and register to vote right after this ceremony. On behalf of President Lyndon B. Johnson, members of Congress, and U.S. citizens everywhere, congratulations on this major achievement, and good luck in the future!"

Immediately after the speech, a woman read the following motion to the judge: "We have eleven petitioners for naturalization from four different countries. I move that you accept them..."

"Motion granted," the judge replied.

At this, Trudi, who had been squeezing Peter's hand in anticipation, slowly released her grip.

The woman who had made the motion then began to read off the names of the candidates. Upon hearing their name, each person was handed a wooden stick bearing a small American flag, after which they were asked to stand and say where they were from and what they did for a living. Trudi and Peter went last.

"I am Trudi Mayer from Ortenburg, Germany, and I am a housewife," a beaming Trudi stated.

Finally, it was Peter's turn. This defining moment was

not lost on him. He took a deep breath before he spoke: "Peter R. Mayer; Memmingen, Germany. I am a carpenter."

"It is a pleasure to meet all of you," said the judge. "Please remain standing as I administer the Oath of Citizenship. Repeat after me:

"I hereby declare, on oath, that I absolutely and entirely renounce and abjure all allegiance and fidelity to any foreign prince, potentate, state, or sovereignty, of whom or which I have heretofore been a subject or citizen; that I will support and defend the Constitution and laws of the United States of America against all enemies, foreign and domestic; that I will bear true faith and allegiance to the same; that I will bear arms on behalf of the United States when required by the law; that I will perform non-combatant service in the Armed Forces of the United States when required by the law; that I will perform work of national importance under civilian direction when required by the law; and that I take this obligation freely, without any mental reservation or purpose of evasion; so help me God."

After the oath was read, the judge concluded with "Welcome to the American Family, everyone! You are official citizens of the United States of America. There's no turning back now! This is a tremendous occasion—congratulations! You have all worked very hard and made tremendous sacrifices to be here. This is now not only a place where you live, but it's a place you can call home. Make your mark on this great nation. Be active in your community. Make a difference. Celebrate your right to life, liberty, and the pursuit of happiness. Welcome home!"

With that, the room broke into thunderous applause, and the new citizens were asked to recite the Pledge of Allegiance. Hands on their hearts, Peter and Trudi stood proudly during the pledge and then during the singing of the national anthem. While studying for the citizenship test, the two of them had had to learn the words to the anthem, and this was the first time they would actually sing it as official citizens. Tears began to stream down Trudi's cheeks. Peter fought them back, as well.

Finally, the judge presented each new American with their certificate of citizenship, and the ceremony concluded.

To celebrate, Peter and Trudi threw a small party at the Cedar Hill Civic Center later that evening, serving bratwurst, sauerkraut, pretzels, and beer—plenty of beer. Peter had also asked his friends from the Waterloo German Band to perform during it.

The hall was filled with friends, both new and old—the Ruhles, Mr. Richter, the Vogels, Mrs. Tischner, the Henzlers, some of Peter's co-workers, neighbors, and, of course, Maria and Harry. Even Peter's cousin Josef and his wife Lena made the drive all the way from Indianapolis to take part in this special event.

During a break in the band's performance, Harry stood up and shouted above the crowd: "Speech, Peter! Speech!" Everyone cheered.

Peter, though he didn't relish the spotlight, stood up and acknowledged Harry's request with a wave of his hand. A hush fell over the crowd.

"Thank you. Thank you, everyone. Trudi and I appreciate all of you joining us this evening on such a special occasion. It's so nice to be surrounded by so many of our friends. You've all been such a big part of our lives here."

Peter then scanned the group and pointed to the back of the room. "Mr. Henzler, you made it possible for me to come here in the first place—and to find work. Thank you so very much! Greta and Hermann Ruhle. Greta, you were one of the first friends I made here. Mrs. Tischner. I would have never known about Cedar Hill were it not for you. And Harry. You and Maria helped make Cedar Hill our home."

Peter paused for a couple of seconds to compose himself before continuing. "There's someone who isn't here tonight that I have to mention. Someone to whom I owe a debt of gratitude: my good friend Georg Klemm. I would never have come here had it not been for Georg. It was his crazy idea to leave Germany to work in America—the thought had never occurred to me before he suggested it. Unfortunately..." Peter's voice began to trail off.

There was no master plan to settle in Cedar Hill, just as there had been no master plan to come to America. Everything in Peter's life had worked out the way it did, he believed, because of God's helping hand. From the moment of his birth and his mother's untimely death, God had guided his life.

"Things happen, and you wonder how they got that way," he continued. "I believe that fully. Things happen sometimes, and you don't know how or why, but they just seem to work out. This was meant to be. Trudi and I were meant to be in America."

With that, he lifted his glass of beer. "Prost!"

ABOUT ATMOSPHERE PRESS

Atmosphere Press is an independent, full-service publisher for excellent books in all genres and for all audiences. Learn more about what we do at atmospherepress.com.

We encourage you to check out some of Atmosphere's latest releases, which are available at Amazon.com and via order from your local bookstore:

Saints and Martyrs: A Novel, by Aaron Roe

When I Am Ashes, a novel by Amber Rose

Melancholy Vision: A Revolution Series Novel, by L.C. Hamilton

The Recoleta Stories, by Bryon Esmond Butler

Voodoo Hideaway, a novel by Vance Cariaga

Hart Street and Main, a novel by Tabitha Sprunger

The Weed Lady, a novel by Shea R. Embry

A Book of Life, a novel by David Ellis

It Was Called a Home, a novel by Brian Nisun

Grace, a novel by Nancy Allen

Shifted, a novel by KristaLyn A. Vetovich

Because the Sky is a Thousand Soft Hurts, stories by Elizabeth Kirschner

ABOUT THE AUTHOR

Michael O'Brien, a graduate of the University of Missouri's School of Journalism, has worked as a communications professional in the financial services industry for more than three decades. His experiences have taken him from copywriter to creative director, entrepreneur, brand manager and political advocacy specialist.

Welcome Home, Michael's debut novel, was inspired by the lives of several relatives and friends. He brings his journalistic acumen to crafting the story, personally visiting many of the places featured in the novel to capture their color and vibrancy within the narrative.

Michael is a lifelong resident of St. Louis. He is married and has two grown daughters.